JIM STEEL:
DIE OF GOLD

D1253972

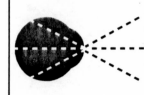

This Large Print Book carries the
Seal of Approval of N.A.V.H.

JIM STEEL:
DIE OF GOLD

CHET CUNNINGHAM

WHEELER PUBLISHING
A part of Gale, Cengage Learning

GALE
CENGAGE Learning

Detroit • New York • San Francisco • New Haven, Conn • Waterville, Maine • London

GALE
CENGAGE Learning™

LIBRARY OF CONGRESS CATALOGING-IN-PUBLICATION DATA

Cunningham, Chet.
    Jim Steel : die of gold / by Chet Cunningham.
      p. cm. — (Wheeler Publishing large print western)
    ISBN-13: 978-1-4104-2308-5 (softcover : alk. paper)
    ISBN-10: 1-4104-2308-5 (softcover : alk. paper)
    1. Gold theft—Fiction. 2. Large type books. I. Title. II. Title:
Die of gold.
    PS3553.U468J56 2010
    813'.54—dc22   2009043700

Published in 2010 by arrangement with Chet Cunningham.

Printed in the United States of America
1 2 3 4 5 6 7 14 13 12 11 10

Jim Steel:
Die of Gold

CHAPTER ONE

Jim Steel walked his buckskin behind a bushy white fir a dozen feet tall and watched through it as the five horsemen ahead worked slowly up the trail. He trained the powerful army binoculars on the five riders, then let the glasses drop to his chest where they hung by a rawhide thong. Why in hell were they taking so long to ride such an easy trail?

The question bothered him again as it had for the past two days as the quintet meandered along the Donner Trail into the rugged high Sierra country. For five men with an important mission, they seemed to be taking their time.

Jim scouted the country on both sides but saw no apparent dangers. The ponderosa and lodge pole pine crowded the trail here as he worked toward the California border. A few white fir sprinkled into the darker green of the pines offered some variety to the heavily wooded Sierra mountain slopes. It was brushy pine country, attesting to the quantity of rain and snow that fell on these high ridges. Alder and willow grew in the draws, and in the open areas, manzanita and sage flourished in tangled, often impenetrable confusion.

The party he followed rounded the bend in the trail. Jim had been keeping them a quarter of a mile ahead, sometimes having to work closer, but never letting himself be seen. Last night he had been tempted to join them. They had surprised a deer on the trail and shot it. The party stopped at once, dressed out the animal and had venison steak for supper.

Jim had resisted the urge to go into their camp; instead he ate his beans and hardtack in a cold camp.

The man on the buckskin stood just under six feet tall and showed lean and hard through his denim pants and jacket. Black hair drooped half down his forehead and hung shaggy and long over his ears. The moustache made a full black slash under his nose on a face rough and weathered from spending more nights under the stars than under a roof.

He shifted his weight in the saddle and felt his mount paw the ground.

"Easy, boy, hold easy. We'll be moving in a bit."

He checked the position of the sun in the western sky. They had three more hours of good riding light left. Chances were they would stop early again. He spat into the dust of the mountain trail. Jim liked this high country. It seemed so fresh and moist after spending so much time in the desert. And up here there never was any shortage of water.

Jim urged the buckskin ahead at a slow walk. This had been a strange job from the beginning. Now he wished he had turned down the five hundred dollars. He was nothing more than a nursemaid watching a squad of mufti-clothed pony soldiers on an easy ride in the sun.

The shots took him by surprise. He jerked his head up but saw no one on the trail. The firing must have come from ahead. He dug his spurs into the buckskin's flanks, jolting him forward at a gallop to the next turn in the trail.

Jim slid the mount to a stop behind a pine and came off in a smooth vault. He ran another ten yards to a boulder and peered around it up the gradual incline of the stagecoach road. One horse was down, writhing in a death struggle. More shots came from the slope to the left. One trooper dodged from a small rock to a larger one, bringing three shots from the bushwhackers.

The army squad was not returning the fire. At least the men had that much sense. He checked the hill to his left but could see no more than could the men pinned down ahead. He needed more altitude. Jim caught Hamlet's reins and walked him down the way he had come for a hundred yards, moved the horse into the fringe of the woods, and tied him. Then Jim began working up the slope to the left to gain a high ground position behind the attackers.

Five minutes later he squirmed up the backside of a boulder and looked down at the battle. He saw only the dead horse on the trail. Then a puff of smoke showed from the rocks behind the horse. At least some of the army party were still alive. He turned his eyes to the area where the bushwhackers must be.

At first he saw nothing, then, from long practice, Jim began scanning the areas best suited to the hidden men. He spotted the first man in blue pants beside a pine tree. A second person moved his head under a gray felt hat and Jim saw him in back of a dark boulder. The third man was invisible until he fired. He wore brown pants and gray shirt, but the puff of blue smoke betrayed his position to be closer to the trail and the most exposed.

Quietly Jim levered a round into the Spencer .56-50 and checked to see that it hadn't jammed. He estimated the distance at three hundred yards and grimly sighted in. For a moment it seemed like it was '64 again and he was wearing a blue army uniform. He adjusted for the range and a touch of windage, then squeezed off the shot.

The moment his piece fired, Jim rolled down the rock and sat still, knowing the raiders below would soon spot the faint drift of smoke from his muzzle. He levered another round from the eight-shot magazine of the Indian model Spencer into the breech and waited. A minute crept by before he wormed cautiously through a tangle of manzanita to his second site. He squinted past the branches of a Jeffrey pine at the situation.

There had been no more firing. Jim could not see any of the army party. Below, sprawled in the open lay the dead bushwhacker in the brown pants. Jim looked for the others. One had moved. The man by the pine was still in place, scanning the hill behind him with binoculars.

"Fish in a barrel," Jim muttered as he sighted down on the second man, being careful to keep his rifle entirely in the shade to prevent a sun flash. The range was a little less. Now he was glad they made him bring the heavy Spencer. They said it was accurate up to 600 yards. Automatically he compensated for increased windage and the fact that he was shooting downhill and fired. Jim saw the man lurch sideways and a rifle spin from his hands. Jim put another shot in the area where the figure had vanished, then scanned the slope deliberately, waiting for the return fire.

He saw the puff of blue smoke and had begun to move his rifle when pine bark beside his head splattered, sending stinging bits against his neck. He aimed and fired three times, bracketing the smoke on both sides, hoping for contact.

Firing came from across the trail as the army men shot at their attackers. Jim saw one military man rise from the brush and run to the safety of a boulder. A slug ripped into his body, dumping him over a log.

Jim watched two more minutes but saw no sign of the bushwhackers. He checked the brush in the ravine and saw enough willow and alder to mask movement by the gunmen either way.

Jim lay where he was, reloading the magazine with the big .56-50 shells, then running a string and round patch through the bore to clean out the corrosive black powder. He pondered the close call after the blue smoke gave away his firing position. Perhaps some day they would invent smokeless powder.

Fifteen minutes passed and Jim saw no movement below. He left cautiously, slowly, not bending a twig, not brushing a limb. When he was well concealed in the manzanita brush, he hurried for the trail below and his horse. Jim trotted in a pace a young Indian brave had taught him.

Hamlet munched on the new spring grass as Jim came up, and didn't even raise his head when Jim scratched his neck. It was time to join the five-man main party and tell them who he was. That had been his directions. Jim welcomed the new action. He had been bored for the past two days. Ever since they left Reno it had been one slowdown after another. This was not his kind of a job.

He had finished melting down and mixing the gold from the gold wagon in Arizona, had split it with ex-trooper Dan Barton, and had spent two weeks of nights and days in easy living. The gold was safely in his account in the Commonwealth Bank of Denver, and he was tired of playing poker.

As things worked out, he had very little choice about taking this job. He would settle that score later.

Now he rode up the trail toward the ambush site with more than usual caution. He was gambling that the third bushwhacker had left. Jim's rifle was in the boot, his six-gun in the holster; he smoked a brown-paper cigarette as Hamlet walked up the grade. It would be uphill all the way to Donner Pass.

He saw the horse in the road ahead and kept both hands on the reins held high so there could be no mistake. The challenge came a little after he thought it would.

A shot blasted a slug a yard in front of his head. He stopped the horse.

"Hold it right there, Mister; don't even wiggle or I'll blow your head clean off."

He did exactly as the voice said.

"What you doing on this trail, stranger?" another voice from behind him asked.

"Going to Sacramento. Isn't this the way?"

He heard the soft footfalls, let the hand take his six-gun, then he turned.

"Now why don't you relax; I'm on your side."

"Pistol hasn't been fired, sir," the first

14

voice said.

"Get down, Mister, but stand easy. There's three guns on your belly."

Jim came down from the saddle slowly, turned and faced the tall man dressed in black traveling suit and string tie. The army man had a moustache with waxed ends that turned up on the ends and wore a white Stetson with the brim curled on both sides.

"I heard some shooting," Jim said. "Trouble?"

"Killed a horse, wounded two men. Did you do the shooting?"

"Why would I do that?"

"The Spencer is warm but the bore is clean," the shorter man dressed in working cowboy clothes said.

Jim felt the tension in the group. He smiled up at the taller man. "The die is cast, Captain Davis."

Jim watched the man relax. He sighed, his shoulders dropped a fraction of an inch, and a scowl charged his features.

"Yes, the die of gold. Glad to have you here, Johnson. Our orders said you'd pick us up two days ago. We've been waiting for you. Where the hell have you been?"

"A quarter of a mile behind you, sir. I figured an outside gun might come in handy."

15

The army horse captain in civvies frowned. "Yes. That was you with your Spencer a while ago on the hill in back of the attackers?"

Jim nodded.

"Thanks, they had us pinned down."

Jim watched as the troopers came out of the rocks, gathered up the horses, and treated the two wounded. Neither seemed seriously hurt. The captain had called him "Johnson." Evidently the party had been expecting a man named Johnson. The nurse-maid job was legitimate, but how could they have gotten the name mixed up? Or had they? Jim didn't like the smell of it. He decided to wait and see what happened.

Five minutes later the squad was formed up and moving down the wagon road. This time they rode smartly and with a purpose. There were no obvious military uniforms or trappings, but the riders acted like troopers under a firm command. One wounded man rode one of the two pack animals they trailed.

The captain had deferred to Jim to head the line of march, and Jim struck out along the trail as if he were set on reaching Sacramento before sunset.

Jim pulled the little band into a grove at the big bend of a chattering creek. There were alders thick enough to use as a fence on one side. To the back a stiff bluff shot up fifty feet, and to the other side a mountain meadow spread out a quarter of a mile.

"Bed down here, Captain?" Jim asked.

The captain looked over the area in a glance, noticed the good defensive position, and let his mouth turn up in a hint of a smile. He nodded and the men dismounted and took care of their horses. Every horse drank first, then had a good rubdown and was put on a picket line in a crop of green grass.

Ten minutes later the captain offered Jim a cup of coffee.

"You ride like a military man, Johnson."

"Kind of a habit that's hard to get rid of, Captain."

"What outfit were you in?"

"Tenth Corps, at the James River. They called it Deep Bottom."

Captain Davis sat on a blanket, his back to the bluff, a cigar in one hand and a coffee cup in the other. "Know the engagement. Pontoon bridge across the James river. Supposed to turn Lee's flank. I had a brother there. Were you under General Sherman?"

"No, General Nelson Niles."

"An officer?"

17

"First lieutenant."

Davis watched him for a moment. "I'm glad you're on our side." He sipped the coffee, then looked up from excited gray eyes. "How do you like all this secret work? Is it as dangerous as I've heard?"

Jim stared at him blankly. "Secret? I'm just an out-of-work cowboy riding shotgun for you for a few miles."

Captain Davis laughed softly. "All right, I'm out of place. I had to ask. It sounds like exciting duty, being directly under the command of the President. Have you talked to President Johnson?"

Jim shook his head.

Captain Davis smiled. "All right, I know when I'm in over my head. I suppose you know all about this particular mission?"

Again Jim shook his head.

The captain threw out the last of the coffee and dropped the cigar into the small cooking fire.

"Just as well, I guess. Neither do I. I don't even know where the blamed things are. They said they would do the concealing. All I have to do is get everything to Sacramento that I left with from Reno."

"So far you're one army horse short."

Davis' face blanched. Then he recovered. "No, they said equipment, clothes, packs.

Nothing about animals. How can you hide anything in a horse?"

Jim eyed the gradually changing sky. "Dark in a minute, think I'll turn in. We'll get an early start tomorrow. When do I pull guard duty?"

"You don't."

"You've only got two able men. Remember we aren't dealing with Indians; these guys won't mind attacking at night."

"I hate to put any guard out at all," the captain said. "The men are tired enough. But I know I've got to. I'll take first watch, then the other two men for four hours."

"Sounds fair. I'll take the point. If anything moves within a hundred yards of me, I'll know it."

"Thanks," Davis said. "Once I get to sleep I could snore right through an Indian raid."

"Until you lost your hair."

Captain Davis stood and stretched. "That's why I don't sleep much in Indian country."

They spread out blanket rolls and slept.

Jim slept, woke, dozed again, and checked the passage of time by watching the Big Dipper slowly circle the north star. It makes a complete rotation every night like the hands of a watch and can give you the time within fifteen minutes. It was almost two

A.M. when he woke again.

Something was different. One of the horses moved too quickly, unnaturally. Jim tensed, his eyes scanning the area, but his body had not moved. He saw one, then two men. One was between the horses cutting the picket ropes. The other man moved slowly toward the guard near the fire. A faint glint of moonlight filtered through the trees and bounced off a knife swung backwards to throw.

Jim's six-gun blasted once, then again, and the knifeman jolted backwards, dead before he could cry out. Two troopers stirred; the captain came to his knees, his pistol out.

Jim lay still, watching the man between the horses. He had to run or ride out. He ran, darting for the alders. Jim fired once; the man stumbled and fell. Before anyone else could move, Jim was dodging toward the man. A shot blasted at Jim. He hit the ground, rolled and came up behind a six-inch alder. He felt the impact of a second slug as it hit the tree over his head. Jim turned and fired twice at the shadow of a man in front of him who started to scramble to his feet. There was no return fire.

"Johnson?" Captain Davis called. "Johnson, you all right?"

Jim moved forward slowly, his hand on

20

the knife at his belt. Just before he got to the body he heard a long sigh, a death rattle. Jim took the man's pistol from his hand and pushed it in his own belt, then rolled the man over and stared at him. Even in the half-light, Jim knew he had seen this man before. He was one of those who had been in his hotel room with Bert Ronson to hire Jim to come here.

Jim ran back to the captain and ordered everyone on the alert. There could be half a dozen other raiders in position around the camp.

After an hour produced no more action, Jim let the other men go back to sleep. He built up the night fire, then went to check the bodies. He looked at the man with the knife. One bullet had caught him in the throat, spilling a quart of rich, red blood down his neck and onto his chest. Jim studied the face, then went back to the fire, a flood of questions in his mind.

The knife thrower had been in the group with Bert Ronson at the camp near Virginia City. He was a small man with a ready smile, and bad teeth, always in need of a shave. Jim squatted by the fire and warmed his hands in the chilly mountain air.

Now he had to know what happened to the real Johnson. It was easy to guess. The real secret service man must have died in some Virginia City alley. The killers would strip him of all identification so he would be another nameless candidate for an unmarked grave on boot hill.

What was going on? What did these men want? And why would he be hired to protect the army party by a group of men who moved in with intentions of massacring that same army detail? And just as important, what was the cargo Captain Davis was delivering?

Jim shook the captain awake. "I've got to have a talk with you, sir, right now."

CHAPTER TWO

Jim had left Denver a month before and worked his way to Virginia City, Nevada, where he heard there was a new silver strike. He had some inside information that turned out to be dead wrong. After a week in the high country, he rode back to Virginia City for a tub bath at the fanciest hotel in town and two days of high living luxury.

He saw a traveling dramatic company perform, went to a bull and bear fight, and won a drinking match against a miner, which took him two days to sleep off.

Now he lounged in the softness of an overstuffed sofa and watched a serving girl spread dinner for two in his parlor room. It was the only two-room latch-up in the hotel. He could hear the steak sizzling on the metal platter.

"That's fine, Miss," he said, tossing her a new half-dollar piece. "Now get out of here so I can eat that steak before it gets cold."

As soon as the serving girl left, Melinda came through the bedroom door. She had changed clothes for the third time that day and now wore a soft white peasant blouse with a low scoop neckline and a black skirt. She bent low and kissed his cheek, letting the garment fall forward.

"How do you like my new blouse, Jim?"

He looked down the blouse and laughed, then swatted her rump. "You know damn well I like both of them, Melinda; now let's eat."

Ordinarily Jim didn't smoke cigars, but as he leaned back after the meal, he lit one and blew smoke at the ceiling.

"Don't know why I spend so much time on the trail," he said. "A nice room, a good meal, fine cigar. . . ." He saw her pouting. "Yes, Melinda, and a good woman. Enough to make a man want to think about starting to put down a tap root."

"You probably say that in every town where you take a bath, Jim Steel."

"Yeah, true." He watched her: blonde hair piled on top of her head over a round, pretty face. She was slender and graceful as a week-old fawn.

He checked her plate. "You eat like a horse."

She laughed and he liked the way her

voice sparkled. "This filly has to eat when the grass is green," she said.

"You won over fifty dollars from me this afternoon in that poker game."

"Darling, never bet against me. When I'm rolling you should drop out; that's teamwork." She shook her head. "Besides, that fifty just brings me even for the week."

"You can always go back to picking pockets. Where was it I bailed you out of jail? Denver, as I recall."

Her smile was secretive, soft. "I had a streak of bad luck, but it worked out all right toward the last. Remember? But I just use the pick for emergencies." Her smile hardened. "You still planning to go to Carson City?"

He nodded. "Some business. A mine up there I want to check."

"Take me with you."

He laughed, letting a touch of desire show through. "I think you'd go."

"Darling, you know I would. We make a good team. I keep telling you that."

"And I'd be there to bail you out if somebody caught those pretty little hands bottom dealing?"

"Well, there's always that chance." She giggled. "Some gamblers simply are not gentlemen." Melinda stood and went to him, bending low again, kissing his lips once, then twice. When she straightened, he held out his hand.

"I don't know what you took, and I knew you were trying. So give it back."

She sighed and held out her hand. "Just a few old gold pieces. Three double eagles."

He took the sixty dollars' worth of gold and started to stand when the door burst open. Three armed men ran into the room.

"Whoa now. . . ." Jim began.

"Oh, Jim!" Melinda cried.

"Take it easy-like, Steel," one of the men with a pistol said. A second man went to the window, the third quietly closed the hotel room door.

"If you know who I am, you know you don't need your gun," Jim said. He studied the man who seemed to be in charge. He was two inches over six feet, sturdily built, with the sun-and-wind-weathered face of a cowman. He wore a plaid shirt, a red neckerchief and Levi's and seemed ready for the trail. The thing Jim had noticed first was the scar. One four-inch-long furrow a half inch wide ridged his right cheek. It stopped just below his eye but made the lid pull downward slightly. When the man turned, Jim saw that his left hand had only a thumb and little finger.

The big man put his gun in its holster, but the other gunmen kept their irons in hand.

"Got a job for you, Steel, but you've got to leave right now. You ready to move out?" The man with the scar asked it.

"No, I'm busy."

"So I see," he said, laughing as he glanced at Melinda. "You been busy for the past two days. We got tired waiting."

On signal, one of the men went to the dresser and began dumping Jim's meager supply of clothes into a carpetbag.

"Waste of time, I'm not going anywhere," Jim said.

"I think you are. Where's your gun?"

"Bottom drawer."

"Go look."

Jim checked. The gun wasn't there.

"Your gun was just found by the sheriff next to a dead man in a back alley. He's got two slugs in him. Since your initials are engraved on the gun barrel, you're in trouble."

"You won't make it stick."

"I got two witnesses who'll swear in court they saw you gun that man down." The scar whitened as the man grinned. Jim said nothing.

"They're here," the man at the window said.

Jim went to the curtained opening. Below he saw the Virginia City sheriff and three deputies swing up to the porch of the Charlotte House Hotel.

"They're coming after you, Jim. Want to work for me? Five hundred for a one-week job."

Jim made up his mind the way he always did, fast. He reached for his empty gunbelt and strapped it on. His boots came out from under the bed, and he put on his gray hat. When he looked at Melinda she was standing almost the way she had when the men came in. A single tear worked down her cheek.

"I'll run into you again sometime, Melinda," Jim said.

"You riding east or west?" she asked the man with the scar.

He hesitated, looked at her again, and grinned. "Try Sacramento," he said. "Look me up." Then the four men ran from the room.

Ten minutes later they were riding out of Virginia City. Jim wasn't sure how they did it, but they had his buckskin, Hamlet, tied at the rail in back of the hotel when they all scrambled down from the low hotel porch roof. The men had done a lot of advance planning, and he was curious about what kind of work they had in mind. It couldn't be legal; he'd decided that. He was curious how illegal it would be.

They rode north for an hour without talking. There was no moon, but they made good time. At last they came to a side road and took it and soon turned off at a cluster of pine trees near a small stream. A man called out a sharp challenge, then waved them into the camp.

"Near given up on you boys, Bert," a puncher by the fire said.

The big man grunted and told him to tie up the horses. Bert settled down on a log and pointed to the spot beside him.

Jim didn't sit. "You boxed me in on a killing. Why?"

"We need you. When the President wants something, he gets it any way he can."

"The President?"

"President Johnson, in Washington. Jim, the United States Government has picked you for a tough job."

"I won't join the army again."

"We know; this isn't the army. We work directly with the President in secret. You've never heard of us, because you're not supposed to. Right now we have a shipment going from Washington to San Francisco. It's due to leave Reno tomorrow on the last leg of the trip."

"Who was the man who died?"

Bert threw a stick on the fire. He didn't look up. "You have no need to know that, Jim. He died on orders. Exactly why isn't your business. You didn't think we killed some innocent man just to persuade you to come with us?"

"That's what I thought."

"I'm surprised, Jim. We need a good man to guard that shipment leaving tomorrow. We want you to do it. The package is with a party of five men. Your job is to be sure they get through to the Bay City unharmed."

"If somebody really wanted to stop them from getting over the Sierras, a troop of cavalry couldn't guarantee they would make it. You've been over that trail?"

The other man shook his head. "That's why we need you. You know the territory."

"I still don't want the job."

"It pays $500 in cash, right now."

"For just a week's ride? That's not the army I remember."

"I won't fool you, Steel. This ain't gonna be no picnic. The cargo is highly valuable; it's in a little package. Say it's worth more than gold. Three outfits have tried to steal it already. We expect more. We want you to move in, contact the army captain, and take them on into San Francisco."

"Will there be any other guards?"

"You don't need to know that, Steel."

"What's the cargo, diamonds?"

"I can't tell you."

"It's a pig in a poke."

"Just be sure the pig stays in that poke; that's your job. When you deliver the party to the address in San Francisco, you're done. There are plenty of soft beds and beautiful women over there, I've heard."

"How do you know I won't hightail it over the next ridge with your five hundred?"

"We know you. You wouldn't do that once you give your word you'll serve as our guard." He stood with his back to the fire and looked at Jim.

"Besides, if you tried it, we'd track you down and put a bullet through your balls, then through your head."

Jim reached down and stirred the fire.

"You see, Steel, we know a lot about you. About that train that lost its gold shipment from a tamper-proof railroad car; about that bank in New Mexico where the holdup man looked a lot like you and kissed the two women as he robbed them. Hear you just pulled some caper in Arizona and came away with some army gold off a gold wagon. But somehow you keep off the wanted posters. We like that."

Bert walked around the fire. "We even know you used to be a town marshall. Got elected sheriff. You also stood trial for murder twice but got acquitted. You're an expert, Steel. The President said for this job we need an expert with your qualifications. And from what I hear you've also got another strange quality for an outlaw; you're cursed with an honest streak that is always getting you into trouble."

Bert sat down on the log, threw a sulphur match into the fire, and watched it flare up. "So, if you say you'll serve with us, we know we can trust you to do the job you contract for."

"They using a wagon?"

"No, five horses and two pack mules."

"Civilians?"

"No, all army men. Four enlisted and a captain. But they all are wearing civilian clothes."

"What happens if I don't want the job?"

Bert's eyes caught Jim's and there was an icy indifference. "We take you back to the sheriff tied hand and foot across your saddle. In Virginia City you'll be stretching rope for that killing within a week."

Jim couldn't outstare the other man. He thought through what he knew about the wild little Nevada town. It was a quick hanging place; he'd heard that. And they had all the evidence they needed. Jim shrugged. Never bet against a pat hand.

"Let's see the money. Hope you got it in greenbacks."

Bert held up his hand. "First give me your word that you'll follow orders, trail the party and see that it gets through to San Francisco."

"Done, you have my word," Jim said. "Now, where do I meet them? What do I use for weapons?"

They were prepared. An hour later Jim was outfitted for the trail. Half of his clothes were packed into the carpetbag and would be taken ahead for him to Sacramento. His blanket roll was provided and his saddlebags stocked with food for four days. The five hundred dollars in greenbacks came in a money belt he strapped around his waist under his shirt. They gave him his choice of three different six-guns and told him to take a heavy .56-50 Spencer rifle.

Jim shook hands with Bert and looked up the track toward Reno and the Old Donner Trail, which was now a full-scale stage road.

"You won't get any other instructions and

nothing in writing, Steel. If you get in trouble and claim you're working for the Government, we won't even know your name. That's the way we handle things."

Jim touched his hat and began riding. He had a day to catch up with the party before it left Reno. He would know them because all five men rode black army horses, and Captain Frank Davis, the leader, would be wearing civilian clothes, a white Stetson, a moustache with waxed ends, and a string tie.

He'd searched for men with a lot less to go on. He'd find them; that would be easy. Protecting them on into San Francisco would be a much tougher matter.

Jim turned Hamlet to the north and began to move faster along the trail. He would ride until three A.M., then stop and sleep until dawn.

The long ride gave Jim a lot of time to think through this strange assignment. He wasn't entirely sure that he believed everything that Bert had said. But he had little choice, either take the job or look at a hangman. He didn't see how he could get in trouble protecting a quintet of army men. It was about time he visited San Francisco again, anyway.

He went over his timetable and decided

that if he made a little better time tonight, he should be able to pick up the party just out of Reno. But he made one change in the rules. He wouldn't ride into the army camp and announce himself. He would hang back, shadow the party, a kind of one-man reserve in case the main body got into trouble. He could serve the safety of the party much better that way.

Jim concentrated on his riding.

The next morning he picked up the party as it left Reno, right on schedule.

CHAPTER THREE

Jim and Captain Davis sat in the shadows well back of the crackling campfire. Jim had told the army man how he was hired.

"So my name isn't Johnson. He probably was the man they shot in Virginia City. I'm not a member of any secret Government force. All I know is that you carry something more valuable than gold."

The captain touched the twisted ends of his moustache from long habit and scowled. "At least you're an honest man, Steel. I probably should shoot you and lay you out beside those other two bodies."

Captain Davis adjusted the army issue .45 pistol on his belt. "But you saved my detail back there from being wiped out, and now you save us again. That was a double-edged Bowie knife. Did you see that thing? So sharp you could shave with it. I've got it in my duffel."

The captain stood and kicked at a clump

of weeds. "Let's look at those dead men again. There must have been only two in that raiding party."

Jim saw that two of the army men were on guard now. It was close to four in the morning.

The first man they both looked at was near the horses. He was the cowboy who had been minding the camp when Jim rode in with Bert near Virginia City. The captain rolled him over and went through his pockets quickly, then checked for a money belt. There was none. The search turned up an old knife, a small crucifix, a plug of chewing tobacco, and a leather pouch with three dollars in gold.

The next man's shirt produced two well-worn letters from home. He had a folding sheepstrap pocketbook and little else. At the fire they looked at the last earthly possessions of the two men.

Captain Davis studied the material for a moment. "This one is from Tennessee," he said. They never knew where the other one was from.

"I'll take care of notifying the next of kin and sending their effects," Captain Davis said.

The two troopers were ordered to dig a shallow grave.

"When they finish it, Steel, I decide if it's for two bodies or three. As far as I know you're working hand-in-glove with these people. Why should I let you live?" The captain's .45 was out, pointed at Jim's chest.

Jim snorted. "Why? You need every gun you can get to go over that pass. Besides, I've saved your ass twice already today; that should buy me something."

They had faded back from the fire so he couldn't see the officer's face.

"You asking me to trust you, Steel?"

"Damn right."

"Would those two men have killed you after they wiped us out?"

"Probably, and taken back the five hundred. That's two year's pay for the average cowhand. This outfit is shooting for high stakes."

"And it's not just for the money, Steel. If they get my cargo, it could mean serious international problems for our government."

"So what's the cargo?"

"I can't say."

"You ask me to risk my skin to protect something, and you won't even tell me what it is?"

"I didn't ask you to do anything, Steel. You can get on your horse and ride out of here right now."

Jim heard the hammer lower softly on the chamber of the .45 and the iron slide back into leather.

"I'll stay. I made a contract."

"Good. Now what kind of strategy do we use?"

"We move at night," Jim said.

"Yes, takes away the bushwhacking advantage, makes it harder to track us." He pointed at the bodies. "As soon as those two are under the ground, we ride."

The moon slipped from behind high-flying clouds as they saddled up and moved out quietly. Jim led the pack, with the men closely grouped.

The wide wagon road was an easy trail. They walked their horses for the first hour, then trotted at alternate fifteen-minute intervals until Jim figured they had put ten miles between them and the death camp. He checked the stars and called a halt. The night was starting to fade.

"Let's give the horses a blow, Captain," Jim said. The man in the string tie nodded.

"Ten minutes, men, dry rations if you want them."

Jim walked to the stream and let his horse drink. The captain came up behind him.

"Were you really at Deep Bottom?"

"Yes."

"And you were a lieutenant?"

Jim nodded.

"Then if I don't make it, you'll be next in command to get the troops and the goods through. I've told them you're an officer, too."

"Then shouldn't I know what I'm delivering?"

"No."

"How about where it's hidden?"

Davis laughed. "A lot of people want to know that. We've used every kind of transport and concealment there is, from river steamer to a single rider, and still they figure out where we are and when we move on." He snorted. "Hell, I don't even know where the package is hidden myself."

Jim turned to check the country. They were in Dog Valley, and it was a straight shot to Donner Pass. Already the outcroppings of hard rock were showing on the slopes. The pines and fir grew in dark patches here and seemed only half as tall as the trees had been the day before. But it was a long way from the timber line.

"How far to the pass?" the captain asked.

"I don't know. Maybe another five miles, maybe ten. We won't get over it tonight."

They rode for another hour, and just as

the sun came up they moved into the small stream and walked upriver for half a mile so they would leave no tracks. They came out of the water and made camp in a screened gully. Jim permitted no fire.

"Anybody following us could smell a fire a mile away even if he couldn't see the smoke," Jim explained to one green trooper. "If you don't want to get your throat slit, just leave those stinkers in your pocket."

Captain Davis sent one man down the trail a quarter of a mile as a lookout. He could see the spot where they had moved into the creek. It wouldn't take much of a tracker to follow their herd of horses up the wagon trail.

They ate cold rations. Jim grinned when he opened one of his saddlebag pouches and found a small can of sliced peaches. He shared it with the captain. Jim considered canned peaches the ultimate in rangeland or rough-trail delicacies.

One trooper stood guard as they slept. At noon Jim rousted them out. An hour later they had eaten, and cared for their horses and were moving again. Jim did not return to the road. He paralleled it, working through the scattered groves of conifers, pausing at regular intervals to listen for any sounds of travel by anyone else. It was after three in the afternoon when he took them back to the road and put the mounts into a fast lope which ate up the ground. They were close to Donner now.

They took one break, then rode again, but this time Jim brought up the rear. He felt there could be trouble soon. If any of the cutthroats got ahead of them and planned a trap, it could be bad.

The back of his neck had been crawling for the past mile, as if someone were watching them, waiting. He guessed any attack would come from the rear, but just when, he didn't know. He was sure Bert wasn't through. Jim knew they should wait until it was dark to move again, but at least this way they could make good time.

They were in big rocks now, with the trail winding around them as it worked toward the top of the gap, which he could see just ahead. It wasn't much of a pass, but at 7,000 feet every foot you don't have to climb helps.

Jim hung back, letting the party move ahead by a hundred yards. He wanted to serve as rear guard. Then suddenly a turn came and he lost sight of them. He spurred ahead but not quickly enough. A horse bolted from a brushy hiding place by a huge boulder. The rider had a shotgun aimed squarely at Jim's chest from twenty feet away.

"Say a word and you're dead," a guttural voice told him.

Jim saw three more men rise from behind the forest of boulders, each with a rifle trained on him. He let his gun hand relax.

"Off the horse, Steel."

The use of his name chilled him. This wasn't just a pickoff of the last man on a ride. They knew him, and that had to mean Bert.

Two men took his horse, another jabbed him in the back with a rifle, and they walked downhill for a quarter of a mile, then angled into a patch of pines just off the trail. A small fire had been started. Two men lounged near it, boiling coffee. A third man rode in, jumped off his horse, and before Jim saw who it was, the man smashed a hard fist into Jim's jaw, slamming him over backwards.

"Steel, you sonofabitch!"

Jim shook his head and blinked before the image came clear. Standing over him was Bert, the man with the scar on his cheek who had hired him two days ago.

Jim rolled over and got up, his head still banging.

Bert drew his six-gun and blasted a shot

on each side of Jim. "Sweat, you Judas, you backshooter. You wiped out four of my best men. I want to know why."

Jim pasted himself back together. "You *paid* me to protect that party."

"You didn't have to be so damn good at it."

"Your men didn't have to be such amateurs. Why didn't you tell me it was a setup? Don't you trust me?"

"Hell, no. Still don't." The big man's burst of anger had cooled. "My boys weren't going to hurt you back there. We had to get a man to the captain fast after we took care of Johnson. They were expecting somebody."

Bert stuffed the six-gun in his holster, but two more hardcases still had guns covering Jim. He had seen seven men so far in the camp.

"We knew you were in town, and we thought you might be interested in this one. But you had to earn your way in."

"What if I don't want in?" Jim asked, his eyes hard.

"You'll want in on this one. It makes your gold grabbing look like half-pint fryin' size."

"You're talking about the U.S. mint dies for the double eagle that are going from Washington to San Francisco?"

"You know about that?" Bert blurted in surprise.

"Most of the fast guns and rough riders this side the Mississippi have known about that two months."

"Those dies are worth millions, Steel."

"Not to me they ain't. I can get twenty dollars and sixty-seven cents an ounce for the yellow. You run nine-tenths of an ounce of gold into a double eagle and some other metal to make the gold hard enough to work, and it's still worth only twenty dollars. You call that big?"

Bert laughed. He roared until tears came to his eyes. At last he wiped away the wetness and the laugh gave way to a snarl.

"The great man doesn't know the whole story, which is just dandy fine with me. And if you ain't with us, you're on their side." He took out a Bowie knife similar to the one Jim had seen raised in the moonlight over a trooper.

"Them were four good men you gunned out there, Steel. We got a close group here. I figure it's time I turn out your guts and let them dry in the sun so my men can sleep good in them shallow graves you dug for them."

As he spoke a rope settled over Jim's torso and snapped tight around his waist, pinning his arms at his sides. Two men grabbed his legs and a third tore open his shirt.

Bert walked toward him deliberately in the high mountain sunshine and let the sun flash off the honed, double-edged blade directly into Jim's eyes.

"Gonna have a party, Jim. A little blood-letting to purify your system. In the process you're gonna tell us exactly where those dies are hidden. Want to know how good a soldier boy that captain of yours is, too."

The blade came toward him, but all he felt was the coolness of the steel. It flicked upward and he saw the money belt severed and pulled from his waist.

Two more men held his shoulders as the shaving-sharp blade bit an eighth of an inch deep into the flesh just below his collarbone and slashed straight down like a surgeon's incision and didn't stop until the knife grated over Jim's leather belt. He looked down in surprise and saw the thin slice bead with rich red blood; it began to gather and trickle down his chest.

The pain came then, engulfing him like the charge of a buffalo stampede, a blurring, gut-wrenching, mind-searing physical shock that left him gasping for breath. Before the glaze hit his eyes, before he grasped fully what had happened, the blade touched him again and behind it he saw the leering face of Bert Ronson.

CHAPTER FOUR

Jim had been knife slashed before, but never deliberately *carved* like a mule deer on a skinning pole. The finely honed blade had seared through his skin and flesh so effortlessly it could only mean a master butcher was wielding it. A steady, firelike pain jolted into his brain with each second. He strained to surge away from the shiny torture, but he was held fast by the four men.

A drumroll of pain thundered over him then, heavy, demanding, trying to obliterate everything in his conscious mind.

The second slash was on his chest from below his chin to his belt. He couldn't look down now, his eyes sealed shut, his jaw upright, quivering with rage and fury so intense that he nearly lost control. No man had ever marked him like this before, not in spirit or body. No man! The blinding, cold-steel terror whipped at his soul, but he battered it away. He forced himself to speak

48

before he screamed.

"If you want information, Ronson, a dead man won't help you any."

Bert relaxed a moment and stared at the blood dripping, racing down the broad chest of the man in front of him. His dark eyes blinked twice, then he wiped at beads of angry sweat spotting his forehead. The big man stopped, touched the edge of the blade with his good right thumb.

"Steel, I'm gonna skin you alive. You made your last big play. Now who's gonna enjoy all that gold you got stashed around the country? Huh? Who?"

"Ronson, you're stupider than I'd heard. You frame me to work for you, put me in that army camp so you can get information. Of course you're too dumb to tell me you'll be having men come in to contact me and help me wipe them out. You're too stupid to let me in on the scheme. Sure, I blasted your four men. They were beginners at the trade. That's what you *paid* me to do. Now I've got what you need, so you want to take out your revenge on me and blow the whole deal. What would your boss say about that?"

Ronson looked up, hesitated, and Jim saw the beginnings of doubt on his face. It was a gamble, but Jim had to take it. He could figure no other reason why Ronson wanted Jim with the army detail. Ronson's men must have killed the other secret service guard before they knew who he was, then needed a fast replacement.

"What the hell information could you have, killer?"

"Like the alternate route for the rest of the trip. Like how good a soldier Captain Frank Davis really is. And most important, where the double eagle dies are hidden."

Again Jim knew he was taking a chance. But he played on Ronson's bone-crunching stupidity to come through again. The movement of the gold dies was the worst-kept secret in history, Jim had decided. But the subject held fascination for Ronson.

Bert held the knife and watched Jim, his eyes suddenly wary.

"Hell, if you knew where the dies was, you'd filched them and gone a'runnin' last night."

He didn't wait for an argument this time. The big knife came down on flesh, an inch from the center slice. The new burning, cold steel bore fruit in a million tiny nerve endings, billowing fury and torture to a thousand brain cells that screamed in anguish. Jim shivered as the third slice on his chest oozed ripe, red blood. His breath came in ragged gasps as the agony grew and swelled and burst on his mind with a sickening power Jim had not felt for a long time. A groan seeped past his white lips.

"Yeah, Steel, suffer, goddamned killer!" Bert's good right hand spun the heavy knife in the air, and he caught it expertly by the very tip. "I'm gonna slice you a hundred times until you come blubbering apart at every joint. You'll beg to tell me everything you got in your guts about that army captain."

Jim struggled to keep his eyes open now, burning them into the face of Ronson. "Better save your strength, Ronson; you'll need it when you meet Captain Davis. He's a good soldier, tougher and smarter than you and your ten men."

"Only eight now, because of you!" Ronson lunged forward, dropped the knife, and slammed his fist into Jim's head, first a left, then a roundhouse street-brawl right that pounded him out of the hands of the men holding him. Jim spun to the ground. Ronson kicked him in the side, aiming for a kidney.

"Wish I had time to give you the full treatment right now, but you'll keep. I'll take my time with you later. Right now we got to catch up with your captain. We got a spot all picked out, open without a stitch of cover."

Two men tied Jim's hands over his head and secured a rope around a sturdy pine. Another line bound his feet, then was looped around another tree and the rope pulled taut. Jim thought they were going to tear him apart. At last they eased up on the rope and tied it so his body was tightly stretched between the trees, with only his buttocks touching the ground.

Jim tried to move. The gunmen laughed. He could twist from side to side, but that only made the slices on his chest ache more. If he didn't move, the pain from the cuts quieted down to a continual roar.

Most of the men were resting under the trees. He heard talk that some of them had been up for two days straight tracking the soldiers.

Even if they all went to sleep or took a ride, Jim knew he couldn't get away. This stretching trick was one the roundeyes learned from the Indians. He'd come across a body once in Indian territory that had been stretched and left. Animals had been at it, but it still hung together when it was cut down. The man had been tortured, then left to die staring up at the sun with his eyelids cut off.

Activity increased at the camp with dusk. Half the man saddled horses and got ready to leave with Ronson. The fire was built larger, indicating that they were well in back of the army group. Jim had been tied fifteen feet from the blaze so they could keep him in sight after dark. Dead branches and an old stump went into the fire, and it soon began to snap and pop, showering sparks everywhere. The men enjoyed the show, trying for larger and larger pops. When they tired of the sport, three of the men went to sleep. The riders moved out, and Jim tried for a more comfortable position. There was none. He was trapped with four of the gang who were going to kill him.

Another explosion of the sap-filled wood blew a large, glowing coal toward Jim. He looked down at it. It seemed to be almost under the rope, over his head. If he somehow could get his arms pressed down a few inches . . . he tried. The guard moved and throw more brush on the fire, then looked at Jim and laughed. He went back to whittling on a pine stick.

Jim tried again. The dampness of the night air helped. The dry rope had stretched a little. Jim pressed down hard with his hands, bowing up his torso to put more weight on the rope. Gradually it lowered. Jim stifled a cry when his wrist touched the glowing coal. It burned, but it was the most satisfying pain he'd felt all day. He tried to judge which way to move so the coal would touch the rope. His hands had been crossed before he was tied. He tried again, felt something burning and held it. It might be working!

Furiously he battered down the pain in his chest and bowed his body more, pressing down on the rope. He moved and pain flared as fire seared his skin. But this time he didn't pull back. Instead, he pressed his hands down harder until he could smell the rope burning.

An agonizing few seconds later the rope burned through and his whole body slammed onto the ground. He looked at the guard. He was nodding. The other three were sound asleep. The guard moved, then settled into another position.

Jim pushed himself up and worked the knots off his wrists, then his ankles. When the rope dropped away he picked up a hand-sized rock. The guard moved again, threw a stick into the fire, and was turning to check on his prisoner when Jim charged. The man had not completed his turn when Jim crashed the rock against his head, stunning him, knocking him down.

Jim gagged and tied the guard, then saw

where the horses were picketed.

Quietly he found his shirt and saw his gun and gunbelt laying on top. He put them on, caught up the reins of the four mounts and Hamlet, and moved them away silently on the soft ground. All of the mounts were still saddled.

He tried not to think about his chest. He needed some bear grease or ointment of some kind. The slashes had stopped bleeding. He had no idea how deep they were, but he knew they wouldn't be fatal. His shirt would stick to them and act as a bandage for the next couple of days.

Jim walked the horses up the Donner Pass trail for a quarter of a mile, then mounted Hamlet and, using a lead line for the other horses, rode. He had no idea how far he would have to go to catch up with the army group or if any would be alive when he found them. He moved at a lope for two miles, then slowed as they crossed the pass and started down the other side.

Soon he caught the smell of smoke. It drifted toward him from the downgrade. Jim moved slower now, watching the trail. It was another two miles before he spotted a campfire, which seemed to be right on the main road.

Two hundred yards from the fire he

stopped the horses, tied them to a tree, and silently worked forward. He spotted two men around the fire. As he came closer he recognized the tall form of Captain Davis. Jim moved ahead without a sound from tree to bush to tree. At last he was satisfied it was only the army party and it was not under attack.

But he was too late. Three of the four horses were dead. Both pack animals were gone, as were all saddles and army equipment. The attackers had looted and left.

Jim hailed the captain and told him he was coming into camp. The tall army man seemed glad to see him.

"What the hell happened to you?" the captain asked, looking at the red bloodstain that almost covered his chest.

"A small problem. I see Bert has already been here."

The captain sat down on a boulder and nodded. "Caught us by surprise just as we set up camp. Had men all around us. Killed two of my men, wounded one, and drove Dillman and me into the woods. When we came back everything was gone, the horses slaughtered and the special cargo gone, too."

"The double eagle dies?"

Captain Davis glanced up and nodded. "Yes. And I still don't know where they were hidden."

"You caught a bullet?"

The captain lifted his bandaged forearm. He shrugged. "Yes, but I'll live, at least until the court-martial."

Jim checked the ruins of the camp. The cooking fire had been scattered, coffee pot smashed, flour spread over one side of camp. A horse's leg lay in the edge of the larger fire and smelled of singed hair and burned flesh.

Jim found a folding shovel and began digging a grave in the soft ground beside the trail. His chest burned with pain at each shovelful. The unwounded man, Dillman, spelled him at the digging.

Before morning broke over the treetops, the two dead troopers had been buried and the camp cleaned up. They didn't move the dead horses. Jim sat beside the small fire warming his hands as the sun sprinkled the Eastern sky with darts of light. He roused the sleeping officer.

"Time we were moving, Captain."

"You know this man, Steel?"

"Yes, Bert Ronson. Told me his name when he hired me. I've got a point or two to settle with him myself."

The man in Levi's paused. "I'll leave four mounts here with you and ride out fast. I can make better time than the four of us together. Maybe I can catch them before they get to Sacramento."

Captain Davis kicked at the dirt. "I've got to get those dies back. You realize that, don't you, Steel? If I don't I might as well turn in my commission."

The captain looked like a beaten man. Jim knew the problem. The army took care of its own, but it also disciplined its own with a heavy hand.

"Captain, I might be able to get those dies for you when I settle my score with Ronson."

Davis' eyes lit up. It was the first sign of life Jim had noticed from the man.

"I've got to get them back, Steel, and I don't have the slightest idea where to start looking. . . ."

Jim felt the old tightness in his throat — the damn sensation when he was going to be noble again. Every time it meant nothing but trouble for him.

"Don't worry about it now, Captain. I've got that score with Bert myself. Still can't figure out why anyone would want the dies in the first place." He swung up on Hamlet and tipped back his dirty gray hat.

"Tell you what. When you get to Sacramento, look me up. I'll be at the New

Sacramento Hotel." Jim frowned, knowing he'd promised too much already. "Damnit, Captain, I can't guarantee you anything. . . ."

The horse soldier sported a touch of a grin around his waxed moustache tips. "Steel, that's good enough for me. Some help, I just want some help. I know a man of his word when I see one. We'll contact you when we hit town. Think that's where the outfit is based that stole the dies?"

Jim nodded, touched the tip of his hat brim in salute, and turned Hamlet down the road. He picked up the trail of the other riders a quarter of a mile on. They were making good time. Chances were they were halfway to Sacramento already.

He calculated the distance from the pass to the valley city. It was seventy-five, maybe eighty miles, as near as he could remember. If he had a string of three horses he could get there in fourteen hours. With Hamlet, it would take the better part of two long days. Jim settled down to Hamlet's body-jarring walk, a steady four miles an hour. Hamlet could keep up the pace all day. With a few jogs down hills and in the cool of the morning, they might make forty-five miles before midnight. Jim Steel sat easily in the saddle and let Hamlet find his own way. It was going to be one hell of a long, hard ride.

Three hours after he left the army party, Jim rode up to the remains of a campfire. There had been no attempt to conceal it or put it out. A few tin cans lay scattered around. There were some cracker wrappers and even an apple core. Now where would a man get an apple out here this time of year?

Jim stepped down and examined the area critically. Off the side of the road he found what had once been several army saddles. Now every seam had been cut with a sharp knife, every piece of leather ripped off, until the saddle was only a pile of odd-shaped pieces of cowhide. On one of these Jim found what he was afraid he might, the clear impression of a twenty-dollar gold piece where the leather had been pounded into the die to help disguise its presence inside the saddle.

Now he knew the killers ahead of him carried the two sets of dies. He still wondered what they would do with them. Counterfeit gold coins some way, but how would that be profitable? If someone came up with a way to counterfeit gold, now there he would get involved.

Jim threw the pieces of leather with the die marks on them in a pile near the road for the captain to find and rode. Hamlet was interested in moving. He must hope for some oats at the end of the road, Jim decided. They loped for half a mile, then walked again.

Hamlet was half ham actor, half horse. He had once been in a wild west show, then worked with a group of touring actors appearing on an outdoor stage. He also towed the company's wagon to the next show stop.

One day his temperament changed and he kept nipping the leading man. So, like any other bit player, Hamlet was cut from the company by the jealous star. Jim had come along at the right time and bought Hamlet for a double eagle and a bottle of shared whiskey. He'd been straddling the big buckskin for over two years.

The sun moved over the peaks behind them, and soon it found the pair winding down the stage road. Jim would have gladly jumped on board the stage if it had come along, but he had no idea how many trips it took a week between Reno and Sacramento. Maybe two.

It was after 4 P.M. the next day when Jim rode into Sacramento. The little town by the river had grown since Jim had been there last. He found a door with a doctor's shingle over it and went inside.

The man behind the desk pulled down his feet and threw a book aside. He was a big man with heavy hands and a booming voice that took Jim by surprise. But his eyes were clear and intense; they gave that no-nonsense bearing a soft lie.

"You sick, son?"

"No," Jim said as he tried to unbutton his shirt. It was glued solidly to his chest by blood. The doctor took another look at the shirt and chest and began to swear. Jim remembered a doctor just like him from the army.

"You trying to die young? How in hell do you expect me to save your scrawny neck if you don't come tell me somebody skinned your belly? How long you been this way?"

"Two days."

"Lucky you ain't stretched out under a blanket of sod somewhere." He scowled and went to wash his hands. "Well, stretch out on that plank table over there; I'll get some hot water."

An hour later the shirt was soaked off and the salve lathered over the cuts. Some of them had started to heal. The doctor tore up a sheet and wrapped layer after layer of the white bandages around Jim's chest and torso.

"Now you get to bed and stay there for at least three days. Then come back and see me and we'll look at you again. No work, no riding, no breaking them scabs loose, ya hear?"

Jim nodded and buttoned up his wet and still bloody shirt, which he had put on over the bandages. It was the only shirt he had. It would be dry in half an hour in the warm, dry air of Sacramento. The heat felt good after the chill of the mountains.

Jim found two dollar gold pieces in his pocket and dropped them on the plank table.

The doctor shook his head, "What's that?"

"Money."

"Been so long since I seen any, I couldn't tell. You best keep this quiet. In this town folks don't hold with paying their doctor. Get you in a heap of trouble." The doctor opened the door for him. "You be back here in three days, or I'll come hunting you."

Jim grinned and went out the door. He patted Hamlet and went across the street to the first bar. He figured Ronson would still be wetting his dry throat in the saloons. The wrapping around his chest gave Jim a fenced-in feeling. As he swung his arms he felt the restriction. He wouldn't be doing anything at full power for at least a week.

After checking three saloons, Jim sat down in the fourth and had a beer. Ronson had to be in town. This was the logical place. And in the hotel room in Virginia City Ronson had mentioned this California town. It could have been a false lead, but he had said it to Melinda with a gleam in his eye. The placer mining had played out here, but there were some hard-rock operations left. This had to be the place. It was ideal for getting gold and counterfeiting — if that really was what the whole scheme was about.

Jim looked out the window and narrowed his eyes. The big man across the street stood by the overhang, then came into the sunshine. He looked up the street, then turned and sun caught a long scar on his face. Jim came out of the chair, the beer forgotten, his hand checking the position of the .45 on his hip. It was Bert Ronson, sure as hell! The man turned into the Golden Garter Saloon. Jim pushed through the bat wings and stamped across the street through a half inch of dust.

It was going to be a pleasure to meet Bert Ronson again, especially now that Jim's hands were not held behind him.

CHAPTER FIVE

Before Jim charged through the swinging bat doors of the Golden Garter, he adjusted the heavy leather gun belt at his right hip where the big .45 Colt hung loose; then he moved inside. He'd seen a hundred saloons just like it. Long bar across the back, double stairs at each side of it, and lots of small tables and chairs for gambling.

He scanned the bar, then the tables, but nowhere did he find Bert Ronson. Jim went to the bar and ordered a beer. He checked each foursome playing cards, then the others at the brass rail, and made one more sighting in the long mirror behind the polished mahogany. There was no one in the big room who even looked like Ronson. Jim motioned to the bar dog with the polishing cloth. The man had recent range work experience stamped all over him from the weathered face to the limp. The ex-cowhand grinned.

"Lookin' for a tall gent who just came through here. Did he go right out the back door?"

"Who?"

"Tall guy with big scar on his cheek."

"Yeah, he was in."

Jim waited a minute. "Where in blazes did the old coot go, anyway?"

"Left."

Jim knew the game that lonesome cowboys play to help while away a long night's herd watch. But he didn't have time. He caught the barkeep's shirt front and twisted it until the face above his fist turned red.

"Where'd he go?" Jim asked quietly.

"Straight through, Mister," the barkeep whispered, because that was all the air he had left.

Jim let loose of the shirt and the old cowhand turned bartender wheezed in a pair of lungs full of desperately needed air.

"Went right through here like a heifer smellin' water. Try the back door yonder."

Jim was moving toward it before the words cleared the man's lips. The door opened directly into the back alley which ran the length of the block. Fifteen or twenty stores also had back doors opening on it. On the other side of the alley were half a dozen houses. Jim saw no one in the lane. Bert

66

could have stepped into any of those back doors. Jim returned to the bar and finished the beer that had been left carefully where he placed it. At least he had some kind of a trail. He moved out to the street and eyed the buildings. Three more saloons dotted the main street of Sacramento down the direction he looked. There was also a bank, a cafe, hardware store, millinery, and a dry-goods store. Chances were that Bert was either in one of the saloons or the fancy woman house just past the bank.

He had hit a cold trail, and he had no idea how to dig out the man. What he should do was start asking questions, but the wrong one could alert Ronson, and that would produce nothing but a bullet in the back. That would be the last idea he'd try. Jim moved over into the shade of the boardwalk porch and leaned against the rough wood of the hardware store. He'd just wait a minute.

Prowl Sanderson glowered at the woman standing in front of his desk. He was a tall, thin man, towering to six feet ten inches, and had once worked on elevator shoes in a circus. He was prematurely bald, with only a fringe of brown hair around the back of his head, and his eyebrows were sparse. His finger tapped his clean-shaven chin as he stared at the girl.

She had been a burr under his saddle ever since he took her on as a bar girl downstairs in the Double Eagle Saloon. But damnit, this was California and it was still 1866 and the calico shortage was far from over. Women were hard to find in Sacramento, and he'd take almost any female he could find who had two good legs.

But this one had been no bargain. He had paid her way over from San Francisco, then satisfied two hundred dollars in debts to get her free and clear. Sanderson powered his tight, hard fist down onto the sheen of his polished desk.

"Damnit, Abigail, why do you get yourself in trouble all the time?" He didn't expect an answer. She was little more than a girl, maybe twenty-two, with red hair, full hips, thin shoulders, and breasts so small Sanderson made her build them up with cotton padding to fill out the dancehall dress.

"Abigail, you've got to do what you're told. It's not your job to tell the customers our whiskey is watered. Hell, every saloon in town waters it. And if Belle tells you to sweet-talk some cowboy, you do it, hear? I don't care if he hasn't had a bath for six months and his breath smells like the inside of a garlic barrel."

He stood, towering over her five feet two inches. After studying her a moment, he walked behind her. When she didn't turn around he grunted in satisfaction, then felt of her soft bottom. He played with it for a moment. She flinched but did not jump aside or cry out. He spun her around to face him.

His slap was soft, chiding.

"Do you want me to beat you, girl? Would you like that? Or should I send a letter to the sheriff in San Francisco telling him you still owe me money? Or do you want me to strip you right here and now and make you earn your keep the hard way?"

He put his hands on her small breasts and rubbed them through the dress. "And for god's sakes wear your tit padding!"

He went back and sat down, watching her face. It was flushed. She tried not to look at him. He could see her lower lip begin to quiver. "Abigail, it's not like you were a virgin. But you're still not used to being felt up and petted a little by the cowboys and miners, are you? Maybe I should put you on the third floor for a month."

Prowl watched the fear and realization grow on her pretty face. She leaned over his desk, her face pleading.

"Oh, please, Mr. Sanderson, no, not that!

I've heard what happens to some of the girls up there. It's just not right. I'll do anything else. I'll do just what Belle says. They can touch me all they want. But please, not the third floor." Tears brimmed in her eyes. She sniffed. Then she came around the desk. "Mr. Sanderson, if you want me to prove to you right now that I'll do what you say . . ." She lifted her skirt and petticoats to her waist, showing her good legs under the bloomers. "I'll take it all off, right now. . . ."

He sat there a moment looking at her legs, at her open invitation. Then he shook his head and stood. He touched her shoulder and turned her toward the door.

"The next time I see you, Abigail, I want it to be a much more friendly meeting." He waved her out of the room, then sat down grinning. Now that was power! God, but it gave him a sense of raw power to be able to control people, women especially. She came in haughty as hell, but before she left she had offered to strip and lay on her back. Now that was control, power! Threatening to send a girl to the third floor was usually enough to bring her back in line. The third floor had only two rooms and was kept for the really rough men, the hands just off the range or some miner who hadn't seen a woman for six months, and some of the locals the girls on the second floor wouldn't let inside their rooms.

It was always on the third floor where he lost girls. An occasional stabbing, a shooting. One got strangled. The girls usually did whatever the men demanded. He brushed the whole idea aside. It was a necessary evil.

Prowl relaxed in the huge swivel chair, bit the end off a cigar and lit it, blowing three perfect smoke rings at the ceiling. He had done well in his ten years in Sacramento. Give him another ten years and he'd have enough money to buy himself a whole town somewhere. "Sandersonville" he'd call it. He'd buy himself a sheriff and a city council and run everything just the way he damn well pleased!

Ten years ago he came to the gold country expecting to get rich quick. But he soon saw that panning and sluicing for gold were not for him. A small store soon blossomed into a bigger one and then a saloon and a gambling hall. He found he had a natural ability with cards and dice. Now he was well toward his goal. The next few days could make the difference.

Prowl smiled. He knew his smile wasn't his finest feature. His face was so thin that some folks said his head looked like a skull with skin stretched over it. His whole body was built that way, large bones, tight skin, and absolutely no fat, only enough muscle and tissue to make the whole thing a working human form.

His brain was lean and efficient as well. Take the Double Eagle Saloon next door. He ran it like a fine clock. The whiskey was watered exactly 30 percent, enough to make top profit and still not get the drinkers down on him. He didn't waste money trying to keep his beer cold. The girls hustled drinks with a lick and a promise for later on, and at the same time those who could be trained picked pockets of obvious strangers and traveling men.

The girls on the second floor had all the business they could handle, and he'd only had one girl killed in his establishment in over a year. That was a record he was proud of.

But his greatest achievement was the bank. The California Commonwealth Trust, which he opened six years ago with a borrowed ten thousand dollars. Today he had a hundred thousand dollars in cash and securities in his bank and loans of nearly half that much given out to area businessmen and miners.

Never in his life had he carried a gun. And he never gambled at the tables anymore.

Prowl considered both rather deadly and certainly foolish. He could hire all the gunfighters he wanted. And since he put his green eyeshade away, he knew that anyone who picked up a deck of cards in his establishment would lose, one way or the other. If the dealers couldn't make the suckers lose, big winners soon found themselves beaten up and robbed or killed on their way home.

Prowl leaned over his desk, removed a cotton stopper from a steamship-style speaking tube, and whistled loudly. A moment later a voice came through the tube.

"Yes, Mr. Sanderson?"

"Send me up a small pail of that clean eaten' ice from the ice house and a fresh bottle of Blue Bonded Bourbon. There's a Miss Lucy waiting there to see me. Have her come along with the whiskey."

"Yes, Mr. Sanderson."

He looked at the speaking tube with satisfaction and put the decorative stopper back over it. It saved him a lot of steps every day. He wanted to put in one to Mrs. Bull's office directly below in the bank but so far hadn't gotten around to it. It was only a matter of buying the proper type of tubing and bending it into the right shape.

As he waited for the whiskey, he checked

the saloon's receipts. For three days in a row the dollar total was down. Something was wrong. Was it the girls or the other saloons in town? His girls were all the best, so it had to be the competition. The other drinking and gambling establishments would be easy to handle. Perhaps one of them could have a fire. He went to the window and looked down on California Street. He saw the false fronts of the stores across the way and down a bit, the Silver Goose Saloon. It was as good as any. He would have it taken care of soon.

The knock on his door caused him to turn toward the sound. "Come in," he said, then deliberately turned his back to the door and looked out the window.

He heard the door open, two sets of footsteps come in, then the tray touch the desk and heavy footsteps leave before the door closed. He waited what he estimated to be a full minute before he turned.

The girl he found standing in front of his desk was pretty. She could be a beauty with some handiwork and training from Belle about how to dress and how to wear her hair. It was blonde and hung in long streams down her shoulders.

Sanderson scowled at her and let his eyes drop to her breasts, then down her figure to her ankles and back up. From what he could see she would be all right. She had soft, brown eyes, a part in her hair down the center, a small nose, and a pert mouth now drawn into a tight line. She was frightened. That was good.

"I assume Belle told you what your duties will be if you go to work with us?"

The girl nodded.

"You know you'll be expected to encourage the men to drink, to drink with them, and not be too touchy about where the customers put their hands."

"I . . . I can get used to that."

She had a good voice, solid, strong. "If some cowboy or miner takes a fancy to you and wants to spend five dollars, you'll go up to the second floor with him."

She looked up quickly. "Oh! I thought . . . I'd heard that . . . Belle said you had regular girls upstairs, that . . ."

Her eyes had flared with alarm, surprise, mixed with just enough anger and shock to amuse him.

"The whores stay on the second floor. But if a man likes one of our dancehall girls and the man won't have one upstairs, then she goes up."

"I don't know, Mr. Sanderson. I don't hold with that; I'm not that kind of loose

75

woman. . . ."

He picked up the paper in front of him.

"Miss Lucy, you were run out of San Diego as undesirable after going to bed with a preacher's sixteen-year-old son. Arrested in Fresno and sent out of town on the stage after being declared a 'painted hussy and improper woman'." He looked up. "There are three more towns on your list."

"At least . . . at least I never took any money."

"Then it's about time you became a professional. Usually it won't happen more than once a week. You should know how to encourage a man to drink, yet not get too friendly. Now pull in your shirtwaist, make it tight across your breasts."

She frowned at him.

"Go ahead!"

She did.

"Now, pull up your skirt so I can see your legs."

"Mr. Sanderson!"

"How much did I pay the stage driver to keep you out of jail, Miss Lucy?"

"Twenty-nine dollars, but . . ."

He took long, easy steps toward her, lifted her skirts and petticoats, and felt of her legs through the knee-length bloomers. Yes, firm, solid, not too thick.

Lucy's face was bright crimson; her hands had clasped in back of her. She began to say something but he cut her off.

"Miss Lucy, we don't ask why you're here, or what you done. We don't want to know what you're running away from. But we know you owe us money, that you're in trouble and need to earn a living. A dancehall girl is the quickest and easiest way, unless you want to become a full-time whore or work in a Chinese laundry for fifteen cents a day. To work for us you meet our standards. Our dancehall girls are the prettiest in town. I can't hire you without knowing for sure if you come up to our standards. Do you understand what I'm saying?"

She nodded, her lips a firm, white line now in her red face. Her eyes stared straight ahead like some china doll, trying not to see him.

He began unbuttoning the frilly white front of her shirtwaist. He was talking all the time now, telling her how well they protected their girls, how they cared for them, fed them well, had the prettiest gowns.

She tried to cling to every scrap of clothing, but he insisted firmly that it must go. A few moments later he uncovered her breasts and saw they were large and perfect with heavy pink nipples. He bent and kissed each one.

Sanderson worked off the rest of her petticoats until she was naked and shivering. Her waist was narrow, with hips flaring wide, ending in slim legs.

He looked at the door. No one had ever come in without knocking and asking permission. They wouldn't now. He caught the girl's hand and led her to a couch at the back of the room.

"Lucy, you're doing beautifully. So far you've passed every test. Only one last evaluation, then you'll be one of our girls." He watched her. She was beautiful, perfect.

"There's still time for you to decide to pay me back the twenty-nine dollars and go your way. I don't want any girl working for me who doesn't want to be here."

Miss Lucy sighed and sat down on the couch. She said nothing, only stared straight ahead and waited for him.

CHAPTER SIX

The widow Hortense Bull paused outside Mr. Sanderson's door, waiting for a few seconds until the watch on the silver chain around her neck read precisely 4:50. Mr. Sanderson appreciated punctuality. She stood in front of George, the waiter, who carried the food tray.

Hortense Bull had been a widow now four years, ever since her man went away to war and never returned. She was just past twenty-eight, had retained most of her girlish figure, and considered herself quite attractive. Lately she had been trying to enhance her natural beauty. She rapped sharply on the door and waited.

There would be a five-second delay if Mr. Sanderson were going to answer. She counted it off.

"Come in," a voice said precisely on the five-second mark.

She went in first, opening the door for the

waiter, who came from the Beefsteak Cafe on the other side of the bank. Mr. Sanderson owned the cafe, too. He was not as fussy about food as some men, but he detested eating alone. Most days, exactly at 4:30, she went to the cafe, selected dinner for him and herself, then brought the food to his office, which also served as part of his living quarters.

"Good afternoon, Hortense," he said, watching her with a touch of humor behind his black eyes.

Hortense decided he must be in a good mood today. She hoped so, as she helped the waiter set the small table for two. The youth caught the quarter Mr. Sanderson flipped to him, grinned, and hurried out the door.

"I'm really not hungry tonight, Hortense."

She wanted to sigh. He never was hungry after he interviewed a new girl for the saloon. She'd heard that he made love to each new one before hiring her. But that couldn't be true, she was sure of it. Not after what he had told her just two months ago.

She turned the cloth back to show sizzling lamb chops, three kinds of vegetables, milk, coffee, rolls, and three kinds of jam, as well as a double portion of rhubarb pie.

He tasted everything but ate almost nothing. No wonder he stayed so thin, she worried. She simply had to convince him to put on a little weight.

Suddenly he stood without a word or a glance at her and went to his big desk. He talked into the speaking tube, and a few moments later there was a knock on his door. Sanderson strode to the door and talked to two men there for a few seconds. When he came back he was smiling. He ate the three chops and the pie, then looked at her critically.

"Now, Hortense, tell me about the business day. Anything unusual happen in the bank I should know about?"

"Just the shipment. It came in by stage with the special courier. It was marked 'legal documents' but seemed very heavy. We put it in the big safe and locked it at once as you instructed."

He bent and kissed her lips quickly, yet with a touch of wanting to linger.

"Hortense, I don't know what I'd ever do without you. Now I have some people to see, but I think I'll take an evening ride in that new rig I bought. Get things cleaned up here for me."

She watched him leave. He had kissed her, kissed her lips! She moved her hand to her mouth and touched the spot, then looked at the hand, as if expecting it to be different. Hortense sat dazed for a moment, not able to stand, certainly not to speak. A wave of giddiness passed over her and she blinked. She had been staring at the table like a schoolgirl. But what a glorious day! Perhaps soon now . . . perhaps another wonderful night. She was sure that he truly loved her. She gathered up the remains of the dinner and hurried out the door. Hortense Bull felt as flighty as a June bride as she hustled into the bank and ordered the junior teller to return the food things.

About the same time, Jim Steel pushed out of another saloon and looked up the street. Three to go. He really didn't expect to run into Ronson again. One happy sighting was more than his share of luck for the day. Still, he had to check out the sin traps. Now that he knew Ronson and his men were in town, he had to track them down, but with as little stir as possible.

The next bistro was smaller with no bar girls. He'd heard the whiskey here was un-watered and the management ran an honest set of gambling tables. It sounded too good. Jim wondered how quickly the other gam-bling house owners in town would run this one out of business.

In the next saloon he found an afternoon mixed bag of miners, cowhands, and locals, all willing to part with some gold or paper money for a drink, the fleeting attentions of a dancehall girl, and some cards. But Bert Ronson was not among them.

Two more to check. He went to the saloon called the Double Eagle, the one beside the bank, and pushed through the doors. It had a small stage at the back and a piano with the front stripped off so it looked like a half-naked woman. A dozen men stood at the bar. Twenty tables showed a glut of card games already in progress.

Six men stood around the faro table. Faro was the most ridiculous gambling game going, Jim had decided years ago. It consisted of a table or board with a layout of the thirteen-card spade suit painted on it in order. A full deck of 52 cards was shuffled and placed face down. Then betters gambled which cards would come off the deck. You picked a numbered or face card. Two cards were drawn on each round of bets so each player had two chances to win. That left the dealer with a better than six-to-one win odds on every bet.

Jim checked the big Seth Thomas clock hanging behind the bar with its gold swinging pendulum. Almost six o'clock and the big room was nearly full. He turned toward the bar and was about to call the man with the towel when someone slid in beside him and touched his arm.

"Hi, cowboy. You drinking alone or can I help?"

He turned and with a jolt discovered Melinda standing beside him. She wore a dancehall dress and a painted face. He hadn't seen her since the hotel room in Virginia City. Her pretty green eyes warned him to be careful. He grinned.

"Why, shore, Miss. Always more fun drinking with a pretty woman. Bring us two beers."

They went to a table in the middle of the busy room where she put the mugs on the table and sat quickly before he could offer to help her.

"Jim, for god's sakes don't let on you know me," she said softly. Then she laughed, a high, loud sound that brought amused glances from some of the men. "Just drink your beer and look bored. What the hell happened to your shirt?"

He sketched it in quickly and she took over. "After you left I got on the next stage coming this way and soon as I got here I found myself a poker game. A nice friendly

84

little four-hander. Jim, you would have been proud of me; I bluffed and I drew a few good hands, and I won the little pots. Then the stakes got higher and I was dealt two aces, kept a king as kicker, and went for two draw cards. The dude bidding against me took two cards, so I knew he couldn't have more than triplets since he opened. I got another ace and I was sure I had a winner. I upped the ante and the dude did, too, and first thing I know he says it's fine to go fifty dollars light. I call and he comes up with a full house. He drew a lousy pair of deuces and blew me right out of the game. He made a big fuss when he saw I couldn't cover the fifty bucks light. Then this tall gent comes along; I mean this guy is nearly seven feet high. Thin as a skeleton too and has a skull instead of a face. He didn't say a word, just put down the fifty in gold and walked away. I had to follow him. He owns the joint, this one. So I'm working for him for two months to pay off my debt."

"Melinda, you sure know how to keep yourself in trouble. Why didn't you lift fifty out of some pocket?"

"They was watching me like a gang of mother coyotes."

Jim was about to give her a lecture, but he stopped. She was a handful, and right then he was happy he had no brand on her sleek little hip.

"You could at least say you're glad to see me, or tell me where you're staying, or something."

"Hell, yes, I'm glad to see you. Especially since I don't have to bail you out."

"Mean I got to do this for the two months?"

"No, show old skeleton nose how you deal and you can cheat your way out of debt tonight."

She stuck her tongue out at him.

"That's some dress," he said. It was bare on the shoulders, cut deeply between her good breasts, and clung tightly to her slender body down over her hips, where it flared wide at her knees into a skirt of flounces and ruffles. Her blonde hair was down, hanging loosely around her shoulders.

"You're prettier than he is, but I'd still much rather see a guy called Ronson, the big gunslinger with the scar who broke into our hotel room."

"Guy with a scar and a bad hand?"

Jim nodded.

"I saw him; he's here in town, but I don't think he recognized me."

"Good, keep it that way. I spotted him an

hour ago, then he ducked through a saloon and I lost him. Has he been in here?"

Melinda laughed and put on her best teasing voice but kept it soft. "Yep, he came in here. What's it worth to you to find out where he went? Fifty dollars?"

"I'll give you two good swats on the rump if you don't tell me."

Melinda giggled. "I like your swats, Jim." She sipped at the beer and leaned closer to him. "Bert must have some connection with the boss here. He's the tall skeleton named Prowl Sanderson. Bert came in twenty minutes ago and went right up the stairs. No man goes up there without a woman unless the barkeep gives an okay. Sanderson's office is up there somewhere. I was in it, but I don't remember where it was."

Jim felt a surge of excitement. Maybe the trail wasn't so cold after all.

"What can you find out about Sanderson for me?"

"He likes girls, I know that. Owns this place and the bank. I don't know what else."

Jim was thinking. He couldn't risk getting her into any real danger, but she still might be able to help. He had to take the gamble.

"Look, see what you can find out about both of them. Don't just come out and ask questions . . . you know. I want to nail down

Ronson, but this might be a way to find out who's in back of him and the dies thing."

"The what?"

"Ronson stole some Government dies used for stamping out double eagles. I want to know what he's going to do with them."

"Oh, yes, that sounds . . ." Her eyes lit up with gold fever. Jim had seen it too many times. "That sounds interesting. Jim, I'll see what I can do." She pushed her beer away, turning with that smile of hers that few men can refuse. "And we'll be partners, fifty-fifty, in any of that bright yellow stuff we liberate."

Jim snorted. "Sure, Miss Midas, a fifty-fifty deal."

They made a date to meet at 2 A.M. when the Double Eagle saloon closed. She would be at the alley door waiting for his double knock.

Jim watched her walk away, mixing and socializing with the customers and, most important, hustling drinks. He stared in open admiration along with half a dozen other men at the way her tight little bottom swished across the room. Just watching that was worth the price of ten beers.

A few minutes later Jim left the saloon and walked a block to where he had left Hamlet. His chest was hurting again, a kind of dull throbbing that left absolutely no room for argument. It was a good thing he hadn't run into the big man with the scar today. Jim would not have given a good account of himself with his fists. He wasn't sure if he could draw his six-gun or not.

He caught Hamlet's reins and took him to the livery stable, apologizing to the big buckskin for not getting him the oats sooner. Jim spent half an hour brushing Hamlet down, filling his oats bag again, then giving him all the water he would take. When the horse was satisfied, Jim paid the stable man for two nights, and when he was sure the horse was settled, carried his saddlebags out of the stable and found the New Sacramento Hotel.

Jim didn't take the first room offered. He looked over the place, then selected a room at the very back of the hotel on the first floor. He explained that second-story rooms gave him the shakes. He made sure the window would open, then signed the register and paid his fifty cents.

An hour later he had bought a new shirt and an extra pair of pants from the dry-goods store where the man insisted that he was closed. Jim picked up another box of ammunition for his hip iron, then ordered a tub of hot water in his hotel room.

Jim settled down into the hot bath, being careful to keep his chest bandages dry. As he soaked he thought about the gold dies. Why would someone want to steal them? Bert Ronson had swung a wide loop to get his hands on them, but evidently he was only a hired hand. If Bert did work for this Sanderson, Jim knew he had a tougher job.

But one point interested Jim more than simply trying to pay his debt to Ronson and get the dies back for Captain Davis. Anyone ready to counterfeit gold coins would need one important commodity for operation . . . gold. Jim could actually do his country a service if he liberated some of that yellow before it got all mixed up in some illegal counterfeiting scheme. Yes, sir, that would be a fine service he could perform for his country. Now all he had to do was find the dies: the gold would be close by.

CHAPTER SEVEN

By ten o'clock Jim couldn't stand being fenced into the four hotel walls for another second. He put on his new shirt and pants and went to the first saloon down the street, where he found a spare chair at a poker game and cautiously moved into action.

He wasn't trying to win, just to stay even. He played steadily for three hours and came out of the game four dollars ahead. He bought a round of beers for the other players, then drifted to the next saloon.

By 2 A.M. he was at the alley door of the Double Eagle Saloon. Most of the lights were out. He knocked two times, then twice again as he had arranged. The door opened and a woman slipped into the darkness. She wore a hood and a long cape. When she turned, he saw it was Melinda.

Gently he kissed her and she sighed.

"Oh, yes . . . now that seems more like the Jim Steel I remember." She grinned up

91

and sniffed. "You even took a bath."

"Two this year. There's something in my shirt pocket for you."

She held up the folded bill she had already lifted. "You mean this?" Melinda opened it and found it was a hundred-dollar bill. "Oh Jim! I can buy my freedom, I won't have to get pinched all day and half the night for a dollar a day." Her smile turned to a frown. "Where did you get it? You said Bert took back the money he gave you."

Jim leaned away from her and pushed his hat back on his head. "I always keep a couple of those sewn into the lining of my shirt or in my boot. Be surprised how many times they come in handy."

"You're a sneak, Jim Steel."

He caught her hand and they walked halfway to the lights in the building at the end of the alley.

"Now what do you know about Sanderson?"

They leaned against the remains of an old adobe wall.

"He's got money, lots of it. The girls say he owns half the town, but he doesn't part with his cash easily. I've seen Ronson up and down the stairs at least twice more tonight. He must be tied into it with Sanderson somehow. My guess is that Bert just

92

works for the money man. The girls seem to think something big is happening. They say they never have seen the boss so nervous."

"They have any idea what he's so worried about?"

She put her hand down the low-cut front of her dress and took something. When she held it up he saw it was a gold double eagle coin. She put it in his hand.

"Warm," he said.

Her eyes flashed. "You bet." Then her saucy grin faded and she was all business. "Is that coin any good?"

He tossed it up and down, then looked at it as well as he could in the pale moonlight. "Feels like the real thing. Can't see it too well, but the weight should be about right. It's a double eagle."

She shook her pretty head. "Have a pocket knife?"

He handed her his after opening the small blade. Quickly she scratched the gold with the knife and showed him the coin again.

Even in the moonlight he could see the difference. The blade had dug a furrow through the gold, and a dull, steel-colored metal showed below.

"Counterfeit?" Jim asked, his forehead wrinkling.

"You can bet your bottom greenback.

There's maybe two dollars worth of gold in the coin. Slick, huh?"

"That's why they want the dies," Jim said, thinking out loud. "In the light the coin might even be hard to pass, but if they had perfect dies, like the ones someone stole from Captain Davis, the coins would be almost impossible to detect unless they were scratched."

"That's for sure," Melinda said as she stretched up and kissed him. She dropped away reluctantly. "Some of the saloons in town and all the merchants are checking double eagles by scratching them. They take only the good ones."

"Flood the country with these counterfeits and it could cause a panic in the gold market and upset our whole greenback economy," Jim said. "No wonder the army and the government wanted to make sure those dies got through to the right party."

Melinda put her arms around him. "Hey, I'm still here. Remember me?"

Jim was more than aware of her as her breasts pushed against his chest. She kissed his lips softly. "Darling, if Sanderson can do it, why can't we? All we need is to get those dies back and buy ourselves some gold and then . . ."

Jim shook his head. "I'm not an iron man.

I wouldn't know how to mix metal to make it come out at exactly the same weight as an all-good coin. There would be equipment to buy, a big stamping machine, and a power plant and then we'd have to find some way to distribute the coins." He shook his head. "Miss, I'm just a simple cowpoke. And I like my gold straight and pure at twenty dollars and sixty-seven cents an ounce."

Her eyes were sparkling again. "Just think, we could take a thousand dollars' worth of gold and turn it into ten thousand dollars worth of double eagles. That beats playing poker all day."

"Forget it, Melinda." He spun her away and let her twirl around. "That's just not my kind of work. I won't stand over a hot forge all day."

"Besides?" Melinda suggested.

He laughed. "Yeah, besides, I've still got that big flaw in my character."

"That ridiculous honest streak that surfaces now and then like it did in Omaha?" She shook her head and walked a step away.

"Damnit, Jim, this is an ideal setup. How can you pass it up? It's perfect. We can hire men to do the work. We'd have our own private mint and nobody could touch us."

"Nobody? Just the whole U.S. army, and the treasury agents, and the Pinkerton men." He turned. "Besides, I promised Captain Davis I'd get the dies back for him."

"Jim, that's crazy."

He swatted her round ass, and Melinda's peevish, pouting face turned to a grin. "Hey, do that again."

Jim took her hand and turned back toward the Double Eagle Saloon. Now he had some facts to work with. He wasn't going in totally blind. His next step had to be to find out for sure if Sanderson had the dies. He seemed like the man who would have them. Melinda might help there.

"You happy in your new work?" he asked.

"Oh, sure. I just love to serve drinks and get drunks slobbering all over me."

"Then get back to work. Talk to the girls, maybe even talk with Bert. See what you can hear or find out. Don't buy your way out of there yet until we get some more solid facts on Sanderson. Can you do that?"

"But . . . but you know goddamn well I'd rather be in your hotel room with you and . . ."

"Melinda, ladies don't swear."

"I don't feel like a lady, Jim. . . ."

He pulled her in close and kissed her. When he let go she clung to him.

"We'll have plenty of time for this after we get those dies. And remember, when we get the dies, there's going to be a few pounds of gold laying around just for the rescuing. Now get back in there and see what else you can find out."

He left her at the saloon alley door and walked away. He didn't look back.

Melinda watched him go with a sudden sense of frustrating excitement. She had never known a man like Jim Steel. He was attractive and rugged and all man in that fascinating, heart-wrenching way. He stirred something deep inside her that she had turned off a long time ago. It was better left alone. She pulled on the alley door of the saloon and slipped inside without anyone seeing her. A few men still stood at the bar, arguing with the barkeep. Melinda picked up an empty whiskey bottle from a table and advanced on the first drunk.

"All right, you poor excuses for men, get the hell out of here; the bar is closed. Joe's got to get some sleep tonight." She made a wild swing with the bottle, being sure to miss the man by a foot. But he yelped as if he had been hit and staggered backwards, falling over a second man tottering on his feet. Four other men left the bar and headed for the door, laughing at the pile of arms and legs behind them.

One man didn't move. He stood at the far

end of the bar drinking whiskey. He nursed the shot glass and stared at her. He was Bert Ronson. Melinda hoped she looked different enough now from when she had seen him in Virginia City. She had curled the front of her hair and set it in bangs over her forehead and had heavy dancehall makeup on. It had to work.

"Hey, you. Feisty witch."

She glared at him.

"Yeah, you with the bottle. Get your fanny down here."

She held the bottle by the neck like a club as she walked toward him.

"The bar's closed."

"I work here," he said.

"Who else says so?"

"The tall, thin man upstairs." He turned and stared at the two drunks who were staggering to their feet, then jerked his thumb toward the door. Both men blinked, looked around at the empty saloon, and reeled toward the bat wings. When the men were out, the bartender slammed the big wooden inside doors closed behind the wings and threw the double bolts. He walked to the bar and began blowing out the kerosene lamps.

She stood in front of Ronson, the bottle still poised.

"The bar's closed," she said again.

In a move so fast she didn't even see it, he grabbed her wrist which held the bottle. He shook her arm until the glass container fell to the floor and shattered.

"That's better," Ronson said. His face tightened and the scar turned white across his cheek. Then he nodded. "Yeah, you'll do. Upstairs, room twelve."

She tried to whirl away from him, but his hand held her wrist and it hurt.

"Mr. Sanderson said I didn't have to —"

"Yeah, sure," he said, cutting her off. "And he told me to take my pick of the girls, upstairs or down. I just picked you. Any objections?" He grinned and the scar strained into a white slash. "Or should I tell Mr. Sanderson to talk to the sheriff about that fifty dollars you bet that you didn't have?"

She thought of the hundred-dollar bill she had slipped into the front of her dress. She could buy out now, right now. But she remembered the die of gold and the possibilities. Maybe she could get something out of Ronson. Bert must know where he took the dies. She seemed to wilt, to give in. Her right arm went limp.

"Now, that's better, woman." His hand reached toward her breast. Melinda pulled back.

"Not down here," she said.

A few minutes later in his room, Melinda undressed slowly. It looked like this was Bert's home. His clothes were scattered around, a dead cigar lay on a jar lid, a picture of a half-naked woman was tacked to the wall.

"Worked for Mr. Sanderson long?" she asked.

"Yeah, you're the new one, not me. I been with Prowl for five years. Half what he got he owes to my help."

"Hope he pays you better than he does me." She still wore two full petticoats and a wrapper around her breasts. She turned to where he stood by the window. She was trying to figure him out, to find a weakness, some way to take advantage of him. At last she cleared her throat. "Is this what you're looking for?"

He moved to her and crushed her soft body to his rough clothes and tried to kiss her, but she turned away.

"Slow, slow, we've got all night." Her hands were busy as she said it. The slip of paper she saw in his shirt pocket vanished into her hand and she found a double eagle in his fancy vest pocket. She pushed away from him gently.

"The girls are all upset. Say the boss's

been mean as hell this week, like he's worried about something. Does he always give the girls a bad time?"

Bert laughed and shook his head as he watched her finish undressing. The petticoat came off over her head.

"Prowl? Yeah, he's got lots of worries. But my only worry is how soon you gonna get the rest of them damn clothes off."

"He's got worries?" she said, throwing the petticoat at him. She put on her best mad act. "He turns me into a dancehall girl for a rotten fifty dollars! I'm the one who gets the rotten deal." She dropped the last bit of cloth and stood in front of him.

Bert Ronson moved toward her, hunger burning in his eyes, his one good hand slowly opening and closing.

She tried to remember what she'd done with the slip of paper from his pocket. There had been no time to hide it well. She hoped he wouldn't see it.

The next morning Jim Steel rolled away from the quilt he had draped over himself on the bed at the New Sacramento Hotel. He had taken off only his boots when he lay down late last night. He didn't feel secure enough in this town to undress. Now he slid into his boots. He fully expected to be a target before the day was over. He'd be bait in a trap, but that was the quickest way to find the gold dies.

Ten minutes later he went into a small restaurant down the street and had breakfast: three eggs, toast, fried potatoes, strawberry jam, and three cups of coffee. It cost twenty cents. He asked a few questions and a few minutes after his meal had settled, he turned the knob on the door of the office of the Sacramento *Clarion.* The building was narrow, barely fifteen feet wide and had been squashed between a saddle shop and the hardware store.

Two fly-specked windows opened on the street and inside a counter ran from side to side of the room with a small space to get around one end. Stacks of newspapers and files filled the tiny front end of the building. A wall a dozen feet from the door blocked off the back shop. The concentrated smell of newsprint and ink assaulted his nose as soon as Jim walked in. Two desks took up most of the space behind the counter. At first he saw no one in the dim light; then to the right a short, dark-haired girl stood and turned toward him. She seemed to be about twenty, with brown eyes that stabbed curiously at him.

"Yes, may I help you?"

As she moved to the counter he noticed her slender form, the conservative cut of her high-necked blouse and a blue jacket that matched her long blue skirt. Brown hair over her shoulders framed her face. Her nose was turned up slightly so he noticed her nostrils. It struck him suddenly that this was a feature most faces did not have. It all made a strangely appealing package.

Quickly he pulled off his hat. "Miss, I'm looking for information about the gold diggings around here. Thought you might be able to help me."

She bobbed her head. "I can and I can't. I'm afraid you're a little late if you want to dig. The forty-nine panning and sluicing has been finished now for ten years. There are a few hard-rock mines still taking out a little gold but not enough to get anyone excited."

She watched him as he digested that bit of well-known information. Suddenly she held out her hand.

"I'm Ruth Wentz. I do the writing and advertising for the *Clarion.* My father handles the back shop."

He took her soft hand and shook it gently.

"I'm Jim Steel." He paused. An awkward silence followed as they looked at each other. The girl cleared her throat. Jim moved a step to the side.

"Yes, nice to meet you. You could look over some of our old files if you think that would help."

"Oh, yes, thanks."

She went around the counter to the files along the front wall. She pointed to one huge bound book that held newspapers laid out flat.

"I think you can find some stories in that one about the most recent gold strike around here. But it must have been five years ago."

Jim pulled down the book and spread it open on the counter. It was filled with issues of the *Clarion.* He went through the pages while the girl went back to her desk.

"Miss Wentz, you write all this, every week?"

"Yes," she said. "But it's only four pages. If we could sell more ads we could do six pages of news, easily."

"Looks like a pile of work."

She smiled and looked away. Jim studied the back of her head, liking what he saw, then went back to the paper. Quickly he refreshed his memory. The sluice work was long since washed out along the American River. A few hard-rock tunnel miners still looked for the mother lode.

He put the volume away and took down

the latest sheaf of weekly issues but found nothing about any dies or counterfeiting.

"Miss Wentz?"

She turned, her face frozen in a frown of concentration. Slowly her face relaxed until large brown eyes focused on him.

"Oh, I'm sorry, Mr. Steel, you spoke?"

"What can you tell me about the story I hear that somebody is counterfeiting gold coins here in California? I hear it may be centered right here in Sacramento."

Her face showed surprise, which she covered quickly. She swung around in her chair and came to the other side of the counter. "Why do you think there is counterfeiting?"

"I happened to scratch a double eagle and came up with iron or steel or something right under the gold." As Jim watched the girl he felt her whole attitude change.

"I'm sure you must be mistaken. There's no counterfeiting going on around here. I'd know about it if there were. And I talked with Governor Low just yesterday and he didn't say a word about anything like that."

Jim closed the papers and put them away. He went back to the counter and stared at her.

Jim pulled the scratched double eagle from his pocket and dropped it on the counter. Then he touched the brim of his hat in salute.

"Take a look," he said.

She picked up the coin, shook her head. "It's not from around here."

"Thanks anyway for all your help, Miss Wentz." Jim took the coin, sure now that the girl was hiding something, and determined to find out exactly what it was, and why.

CHAPTER EIGHT

Jim had just crossed California Street when he saw three riders come into town. The first was Captain Frank Davis with his two pony soldiers behind them. Frank was dirty, bearded, sitting low in the saddle from the hard ride. One of the enlisted men who was not wounded brought up the rear. There was no doubt they were army, even though they were not in uniform. They rode directly to a doctor's office and went inside.

Jim was sure the captain saw him as he passed, but he made no sign of recognition. Jim went back to the rocking chair in front of the hardware store and waited for half an hour; then he walked across the street into the doctor's office where the army men were.

Captain Davis was pacing the floor as Jim came in. The doctor worked on a man in the next room, trying to repair one of the trooper's legs. The captain had a fresh bandage on his arm. When Jim's eyes met the captain's, he saw the despair and exhaustion. The captain had pushed beyond his endurance.

Jim went to him where the doctor couldn't see them.

"Come to room seven, New Sacramento Hotel," Jim said, then left. There was no advantage in making it known that he was acquainted with the military group. And secrecy now might be helpful later on.

Jim flexed his gun hand as he went across the street and down to the hotel. He was feeling better, but he wouldn't want to draw quickly. Any sudden backward movement with either hand sent a blistering gush of pain through his chest. It might be a month before that was healed properly. The memory of the three slashes down his chest brought a new surge of anger. He fought it down, knowing he had to wait for his confrontation with Ronson. Now simply wasn't the time. But there would be a time; he would see to that.

Jim was waiting for the army man when the captain knocked on his door at the hotel.

"Yes?"

"Davis."

Jim opened the door, let the man in, then closed and locked it.

"You look tired, Captain."

Davis sat down in the chair and winced as he pulled his arm around. "Yes, Steel, tired, angry, and worried. I've got to get those dies."

"Now I know why," Jim said, tossing him the scratched double eagle. He went on to fill in the army man on all that had happened since they parted, the counterfeiting, Ronson, and the possibility that Sanderson was the man they were after.

"Then let's move in and clean him out," Davis said.

"We can't, Captain. He's got a dozen guns in there and we have two and a half. We haven't any court order, no search warrant, no proof even that he has the dies. And you can bet your last greenback he doesn't have them in the saloon."

"I'll have help soon," the captain said. "I telegraphed the Presidio for a detachment of men, horses, and money. They'll be here in two days."

"Then let's wait for two days and do some scouting and planning."

Captain Davis nodded. "I guess that's all we can do." He moved the wounded arm and winced. "Damn arm is giving me trouble. Never had a gunshot hurt so much." He slammed his fist down on the

109

chair. "Damnit, if there were only something I could do!"

Jim saw that the captain was so trail-weary he would be worthless for the next few hours. His waxed moustache sagged on each end; his broadcloth suit was torn and dirty. He looked ready to collapse.

Jim talked the captain into taking a room at the hotel, having a hot bath, and getting some new clothes. His uniform would come with the troop detachment, he said. It was almost noon when Jim got the captain situated and left him to his tub of hot water.

Right after lunch Jim talked to the hardware store clerk about mining supplies. The newspaper had listed only two mines as still working. Jim got their approximate locations and thanked the merchant.

Next he wanted to go into the Double Eagle Saloon and talk to Melinda, but most of the girls didn't start work until four o'clock, so that would have to wait. Instead he went back to the hotel to check on the captain. As he passed the clerk's desk he noticed an envelope sticking out of his pigeonhole room number. The clerk handed it to him, and Jim strolled outside to the wide porch and sat in a rocking chair as he opened the envelope and found a note. It was from Melinda: "Picked this off Ronson last night. Don't know what it means. See me tonight, same time and place."

He looked at the folded yellow paper and the series of words that were written there. They were not sentences: "Gradeout, Ten, Fifteenth, Ten Percent, Diamondback, 6:30 A.M. Blunderbuss."

Jim rocked in the chair for a few minutes trying to make some sense out of the riddle. Someone had written the note in code, or perhaps it had no real meaning. It could be a simple list of items to jog someone's memory. But as he studied the words again, some of them had possible tie-ins. Today was June 14. Tomorrow was the fifteenth. Could it mean something was to happen tomorrow about the gold dies? Ten percent could refer to ten percent gold to be used on the coins. The other words seemed to be unrelated. He looked down the dry, dusty street, a slow fury building in him. Here he had something in his hands that might unlock the secret behind this whole die-stealing plot, but he couldn't decipher it. He got up and stomped down the sidewalk, heading for the Double Eagle Saloon. Maybe now was the time for his confrontation with Bert Ronson.

Jim never got there. He was just passing the hardware store when he felt a rush of air past his head and a fraction of a second later heard the snarl of a hand gun. Jim dropped to the boardwalk and rolled behind two iron stoves set up on display. The shot came from across the street and Jim spotted the location, the open alley mouth between two saloons. Another slug hit the front of a stove and whined off into the distance. Jim's colt came into his hand and he fired around the side of the stove at the lingering puff of blue smoke close to the ground near the alley building. Jim fired again, and when there were no answering shots bolted for a wagon twenty feet away which would give him a clear view down the alley. He made it without being fired at, and when he looked into the alley, it was empty.

Jim resisted the urge to rush after the culprit. It would be an ideal spot for a trap with bushwhacking guns on both sides of the alley waiting for him. He put his gun back in leather.

When Jim looked down the boardwalk, a man was jogging toward him. Jim tensed and was about to draw when he saw the glint off a badge on the man's chest.

"Trouble?" the man asked as he stopped in front of Jim "We don't allow no shooting in the city limits."

"Bushwhacker, Sheriff. Tried to gun me

down from across the street there."

The sheriff glanced at the spot and the distance. The lawman was six inches shorter than Jim and wore two guns. Jim wondered if he could use either one. He wore a fancy vest, forty-dollar boots, and a fine broadcloth gray suit. Jim checked the soft skin on his face and knew the sheriff didn't spend many nights under the stars. He was a soft, stay-at-home type who made his deputies do the dirty work and make the long rides.

" 'Pears as if he wasn't too serious about killing you, mister. We ain't got nobody in the county could hit you with a hand gun from over there."

"When slugs come whistling past me that close, Sheriff, I don't ask for invitations; I shoot back."

The sheriff turned and sent a squirt of black tobacco juice into the dust of the street. "Mister, I'm Ambrose Miller, sheriff of Sacramento County. We got laws here that say no shooting in the city limits. I see you discharge that weapon of yours again, I'll be forced to take it away from you till you leave town."

"Just be sure you tell that to the guy who shot at me," Jim said. He turned his back on the sheriff and walked toward the hotel. He wanted to smile as he left. The bait was spread; somebody knew he was in town and Jim could bet it was Bert Ronson. He went into the New Sacramento Hotel and asked for his key.

"Sure hope you can keep things quiet around here for a spell. I've got to catch up on some sleep," Jim said in a voice loud enough to carry. "You let things get noisy out here and you'll answer to me."

A dozen eyes followed his progress as he went to his first-floor room in the back. He checked the window to make sure it would slide up and down easily and settled down to wait.

A half hour later Jim heard sounds outside his ground-floor window. A man could stand on the ground and look over the sill. Jim tensed but didn't move. He held his breath as he heard the window ease up slowly. Then a gun came over the window ledge and fired three times into the form under the blanket on the bed.

Jim lunged away from the wall beside the window where he had been waiting and jammed his own revolver out the opening. He aimed at the running form and fired three times so fast it sounded like one big explosion. The man in the alley stumbled as his right leg crumpled and he fell hard in the dust, his gun sliding away from him.

Jim pushed through the window and ran to the spot where the gunman had fallen. He kicked the gun farther into the weeds. The man was slender and unshaven; he was lying on his stomach. Jim booted him in the side, drawing a moan as the man rolled over on his back. Jim's .45 went into the man's mouth past protesting lips and a strangled cry.

"Why?" Jim snarled. "Tell me why you tried to gun me down in my bed or I'll blow off the top of your head." Jim pulled the blued-steel muzzle from the man's mouth.

"They told me to, gave me ten dollars. . . ."

"Who told you to?"

"Told me to kill you, to make sure, that you were sleeping in your room, like shooting fish in a bucket. . . ."

Jim kicked him again and thumbed back the hammer on his Colt, cocking it.

A shot blasted the dust between Jim's boots. He looked up and began to lift his gun when he saw the sheriff walking toward him. One deputy held a shotgun and the other was levering a new round into a Henry repeater rifle.

"Just stand easy, son, we got you covered dead to rights."

"This time I'm glad to see you, Sheriff.

Some saddlebum tried to drygulch me when I was sleeping in my hotel bed."

"That a fact? You got any witnesses, son?" The sheriff bent and examined the bushwhacker's shot-up leg, then looked at Jim.

"Yeah, a blanket and some pillows shot full of holes; they should make good witnesses."

"Them don't count, son. What happened?"

"I figured somebody would try for me, so I put a roll of blankets in my bed and hid beside the window. After he shot, I leaned out the window and threw some lead at him and one got him in the leg."

"True, you shot him. My deputy saw you shoot this man. Deputy Mauser here was walking down the alley behind this man and suddenly, without reason or just cause, you leaned out your hotel room window and gunned him down. Man didn't have a chance — didn't even have his gun out, near as I can see."

Jim still hadn't lifted the muzzle of his .45. Now it was too late. Both the long guns pointed at his belly.

"No problem, son, you'll get a fair trial. This is California and we got laws here. Just give me your weapon and come along peaceable. I'm arresting you for the attempted murder of this pore soul in the dirt here."

CHAPTER NINE

A dozen more persons, attracted by the gunshots, gawked at the small procession as Sheriff Miller led Jim around the corner of the hotel. Jim saw Ruth Wentz at one side staring at him. She motioned to him and whispered something, but Jim couldn't understand. If she wanted to tell him anything, she'd have to say it out loud. She frowned.

Speaking evidently was exactly what she didn't want to do. She tried again, mouthing the words, flipping her long brown hair in anger before she ran ahead of the group and tried again.

Jim would have grinned at her futile efforts if he weren't so concerned about his situation. It was a gunslinger frameup if he'd ever seen one. He knew lawmen sometimes used the trick to get rid of a fast gun in town who was vicious as a rattlesnake but couldn't be touched legally.

The plan was to send out a drunk to try to bushwhack the gunman. If the drunk got the gunnie, the town was better off and the killer got a free bottle. If the gunshark shot the drunk, the law arrested him for that and hung him, put him in prison, or ran him out of town. Neat and highly effective. Now he was on the wrong end of the play.

His gun was gone, and he wasn't going to argue with a twelve-gauge scattergun, especially not at point-blank range. He didn't want two hundred birdshot in his gut.

Miss Wentz gave one more try to make him understand, then frowned prettily in defeat as they turned the corner, walking toward the city jail.

"All right, move back there, let us through," Sheriff Miller called out as they passed two saloons which had emptied out at word of a gunfight. "Excitement's all over, folks, git on about your doings."

Half a block to go, then Jim knew his chances would be zero to none. Right now they were little better. The sheriff walked ahead, the armed deputies in back. He could take out one gunman with a jumping kick to the stomach, a trick he'd learned from a Chinaman, but the other deputy would blast him half a second later. The odds were too long.

They moved from the dust of the street to the boardwalk with only three more buildings to pass before coming to the jail. Jim twisted his face into a scowl. He'd let himself get suckered into a trap and there wasn't a damned thing he could do about it. As they passed the Silver Dollar Saloon, the doors jolted open and three drunks reeled out. The first stumbled into the sheriff, knocking him flat. The other two blundered at the same instant into the two deputies.

"Hey, goddamnit . . ."

It was all the lawman had a chance to say before he crumpled onto the boardwalk, the drunks somehow flopping on top of every gun in sight. Jim caught a quick glance at the man who had knocked down the sheriff; it was Captain Davis. The soldier pointed at the alley and Jim sprinted for the opening. Just out of sight he found Hamlet saddled and ready to ride. A boy held the reins. Jim vaulted into the saddle and kicked the big buckskin into motion before the boy knew what happened.

"Hey, where's my nickel?" the kid yelled.

By that time Jim was halfway down the alley, riding hard. He expected a slug from the Henry repeater to tear into him or Hamlet at any time, but none did. He cleared the end of the alley and galloped at full speed out of town. A half mile later, Jim eased off when he passed the last house. He slowed to a jog and watched behind him, but there didn't seem to be anyone chasing him.

Jim rode a mile more to the west, dismounted at the edge of a small stream. Hamlet worked on some grass as Jim had a drink from the clear creek, then sat with his back against an oak tree as he waited for dusk to close in. It would be dark in an hour; then he had to get back into town and try to find out what Ruth Wentz was so interested in telling him.

Jim closed his eyes, but he didn't sleep. He had that automatic and cultivated sheen of the alertness of a hunted animal which protected him. He would have heard a horse half a mile away or a footfall on the soft bank of the stream a hundred yards from him.

Nothing disturbed Jim for an hour; then he came to his feet as he thought of Melinda. For a moment he wondered how she was getting along at the Double Eagle Saloon. Not that he worried about her, for Melinda had proved herself to be tough and ingenious when it came to looking out for herself. She was a confidence expert of the very first water.

But Ruth Wentz continued to puzzle him. If she knew anything about what was going on in Sacramento, she must have heard about the counterfeiting. But as soon as he mentioned it, she cut him off. He sighed. She was an attractive woman, but perhaps she too was under the thumb of Prowl Sanderson. Stranger things had happened. He'd seen a dozen small Western towns where the newspaper had either been bought off or burned out. Here in Sacramento his suspicions were strongly bent toward the former method. If so, why would she not be willing to come forward in front of the sheriff and talk? But if Prowl had bought off the newspaper owners, he surely would own the sheriff too. Jim's frameup supported that.

Just after dark Jim rode to the outskirts of Sacramento and spent ten minutes under a big oak tree's low-lying branches, watching the streets. It was Tuesday night and quiet. He spotted no guards, no patrols, no men lying in wait. Jim rode cautiously up the first street, down a dozen blocks, and then into what he was sure was the alley in back of the small newspaper office. He tied Hamlet at a hitching post at the end of the alley.

There were buildings on one side of the access and only a few houses across the alley. Room for expansion, he decided, provided for the future by some long-sighted city official.

Jim moved from shadow to shadow along the backs of the buildings. The moon was out full, and the light became a problem for him. Every few steps he paused and listened, then watched his back trail and the way forward before he moved again. It took him twenty minutes to cover the half block to the small door with one word printed on it, "*Clarion.*"

Gently Jim tried the door. Locked. He thought of using his knife to open the simple lock, then decided he might meet a shotgun blast. He knocked. Then he rattled the door. At last he pounded on the panel with his boot heel.

If this little newspaper were like dozens of others, there would be living quarters in back or upstairs. He knocked again and this time heard movement. A moment later the lock clicked, then he heard a heavy bolt being drawn back and a six-gun came out the doorway as it opened a crack.

"Who is it?" a woman's voice asked.

"Jim Steel."

The door swung wide at once and Ruth

Wentz motioned him inside. She held a lamp, and he saw she wore a long robe; her hair had been put up in curling papers and covered with a small shawl. She didn't offer any apologies or seem embarrassed by her appearance.

"I heard you got away," she said. Then a flash of concern came to her green eyes. "Are you safe here?"

He took the lamp and nodded. "Safe as any place in town, Miss Wentz. You tried to tell me something today when I was a guest of the sheriff. I couldn't make it out."

"Oh, yes. My mother was deaf and I always formed words with my mouth to her without saying them. I thought you might be able to understand me. I was trying to tell you I was sorry. I probably could have prevented your arrest."

They had moved from a storeroom onto a stairway that led to a set-back second story. At the top of the stairs Jim found a living area with two kerosene lamps burning and a stew bubbling on a wood cook stove.

"Have you had supper?"

He shook his head. Without waiting for his approval she ladled out a big plateful of stew and set it at the side of a small table. Two plates had already been used there. She brought silverware and moved a chair for him.

"Coffee?"

He nodded. When he sat down he smiled. "I really didn't come asking for a handout, but it looks good."

"Jim, I lied to you today," she said suddenly from across the table. "I told you I hadn't heard about the counterfeiting. That was a plain, unforgivable lie. I should have told you a lot about this town, and about Sheriff Miller and Prowl Sanderson. . . ."

Jim forked a carrot into his mouth and chewed it.

"I can guess a lot of it. Sanderson is running the town. He owns the sheriff. For a while I thought he had bought off your paper here as well." He laughed, then sipped the strong black coffee. "But now I see he didn't. So you're fighting against him?"

"Yes, for as long as we can. He ran out the former paper owners here, forced them to sell."

"And you were surprised that you could buy the plant and the building so cheaply?"

"True."

"It's happened a hundred times, Miss Wentz —"

"Ruth, please call me Ruth."

He nodded. Her nose quivered and he noticed again how tipped up it was.

"Ruth, some men think they can buy anything they want. If money doesn't work a gun is next. You don't look like the kind of a woman who would permit that."

"Oh, Prowl tried. First he came to court me. I couldn't stand to be in the same room with him. And when I found out he runs the fancy woman house too, I told him to get out and never come back. Next he tried to buy me out. Claimed he had his own editor. The people of Sacramento deserve one paper that's not slanted by anyone's money. So we refused. Then last week on the sidewalk he stopped me and threatened to ruin us if we said anything disrespectful about him. I went right to the attorney general at the statehouse and got an injunction from the court against him. Then I put his threat into the court record. That really made him mad, but he doesn't have any control over the state people."

"Did that slow him down?"

She shook her pretty head, green eyes angry. "No, but at least he hasn't burned us out."

"We'll try to stop him from doing that."

She watched him eat the stew and butter another slice of bread. She stood as if trying to lift her courage.

"Jim."

He glanced up.

"I'm going to print a story about the counterfeiting. The governor asked me not to use it until we had something solid. Now I have and I'm going ahead, I'm not sure what your connection is with all this."

He told her about the stolen dies and his pledge to the captain to get them back. Jim said nothing about Melinda.

"Now what else do you know that I don't?" Jim asked.

She wrinkled her brow and walked around her chair. Jim enjoyed watching her. Pretty girls in the West, especially the sections he'd been in lately, were as scarce as hen's teeth.

"Not much. The army is sending in a group of men to help search for the dies. Nobody knows who is doing it."

"Could it be Sanderson?"

She lifted her eyes and nodded. "Yes; yes, it might be. But he has so much to risk that I doubt it."

They both heard the pounding on the back door at the same time. She held up her hands in surprise.

"Let's both go see who it is," Jim said.

Downstairs at the back door the knocking came again, and the girl shouted a question through the thick wood. Only a muffled voice came back. Jim started to draw his six-gun, then realized the sheriff still had it. He pointed to his empty holster and the girl moved to one side and brought back a Sharps single-shot rifle. He tried the bolt of the gun until he saw it was loaded, then nodded for her to open the door.

Jim had set the lamp down when he took the gun, and as the door came open, the figure of a man was in heavy shadow. For a split second Jim thought he recognized him and Jim lowered the end of the rifle. At the same time the man in the shadows lifted his revolver and put it against the girl's head.

"Drop the rifle," the voice said.

Jim knew it would discharge if it fell on the floor. Instead, he put both hands on the barrel and passed it carefully to the figure still in the darkness.

CHAPTER TEN

The man-shadow took the rifle from Jim.

"All right now, stand easy, both of you."

It was a command, and the lilt of the voice and the army term tied it together for Jim.

"You can put down your iron, Captain Davis," Jim said. "We don't know the password, but we're friends."

They heard a snort from the darkness. Slowly Jim lifted the lamp so the person outside could see both of them.

The visible six-gun muzzle moved downward and Jim heard the hammer lower softly on the firing chamber. Captain Frank Davis stepped into the circle of lamplight.

The captain's moustache was freshly waxed, the ends now extended an inch on each side of his lips with an upward twist. He wore new civilian clothes, a new conservatively cut jacket and trousers that almost matched. Davis looked at the girl with surprise as he stepped into the light.

The captain shook hands with Jim, then turned to Ruth, saluted stiffly, and bowed. "Begging your pardon, Miss, I'm Captain Davis."

She smiled. "Yes, Captain, I'm Ruth Wentz and that's the first time I've ever been saluted."

"Sorry to break in like this, but Jim had been here too long, and I was concerned . . . I mean he's very important to our plans . . . that is, I really need him."

Jim laughed at the captain's unease in the presence of a pretty girl.

"How did you know I was here?" Jim asked.

The captain smiled. "We knew which way you took out of town, so we covered the three main streets leading back in. We figured we'd spot you."

"Three? You've got a man on sick call."

"We got a volunteer."

Jim nodded, remembering the boy who held his horse in the alley. "Yeah, and I owe him a nickel." Jim turned back to Ruth. "Another question. From what I read in your paper there are only two hard-rock mines still working around here. Does Sanderson own one of them?"

Ruth thought back. Slowly she shook her head. "Not as far as I know. There's nothing on record about it anyway. And I've never heard of any purchase."

"What about foreclosure; he owns the bank, doesn't he?"

Again she shook her head.

"He still might have control of one," Jim said. "A kind of silent partner. I've been thinking about the counterfeiting. It isn't an easy process. Some damn big machine has to stamp out those coins. A hard-rock mine would be a great coverup. They have buildings, and probably a stamping mill of some kind, and steam engines for power, water for cooling. It would be ideal."

"Both mines are up on the Auburn Ravine on the middle fork of the American River," Ruth said. "It's quite a ride to get there. The whole area used to be full of Long Tom sluice boxes and panners, but that's been done with for years now."

Jim walked toward the outside door, then back. "How many of the counterfeit double eagles have turned up so far?"

Ruth paused, remembering, and he enjoyed just watching her.

"The sheriff said he has four; the state attorney general turned over twenty to the federal people. But there must be dozens more around people won't turn in because they lose the twenty dollars."

"So Sanderson or someone had to have a place to make at least a couple of hundred. He couldn't do that here in town, could he?"

Ruth shook her head.

"I haven't seen anyplace where that kind of noise could be hidden," Captain Davis said. "A telegram I got today from San Francisco said the government estimated there were three hundred of the coins made. Some have shown up in the bay area and as far south as Los Angeles."

Jim turned suddenly for the door as he had done a thousand times, but now the movement brought a gasp of pain.

"Jim, are you hurt?" Ruth asked.

Captain Davis suppressed a grin. "Jim? Why, no, Miss, he's just barely scratched, right?" He touched his hat again in a salute. "Miss Wentz, I'll check on the horses. Jim, I hope to see you outside in a moment."

He turned and went out the back door silently.

"Now there is one hell of a fine man," Jim said.

She glanced up at him. "Yes, he does seem nice. But why did he leave so suddenly?"

Jim moved toward the girl and smiled. "He wanted to give me a chance to kiss you goodbye." He took her pretty face in his hands and kissed her unprotesting lips. She swayed toward him until their bodies touched for just a second; then she pulled back.

"Jim, I . . ."

"Yeah, Ruth, me, too. . . ." He let go of her. "Guess I better get out there and look over a couple of mines. Don't you go away anywhere. I've got some things to talk over with you."

Before she could answer, he put a finger across her lips. At the door he paused. "Could I borrow that six-gun you had when I came in? The sheriff still has mine."

She took it from a shelf and handed it to him. It was a Colt .45. He liked the feel of it. Jim checked to see that the five chambers were filled, leaving the one under the hammer empty.

"I'll be back," he said and went out.

Jim paused outside the door until he heard the heavy bolt slide home; then he moved cautiously down the alley to the street and spotted Davis with the two horses. One of them was Hamlet.

"You're a good man, Captain. I may recommend you for promotion."

"It'll be a court-martial instead unless we can get those dies. You think one of those mines might be the spot?"

"I hope so."

"Why don't we raid the saloon first? We might save a long ride."

Jim shook his head. "He's still got too many guns in there, and about fifteen women, including Melinda. Anyway, if I owned a bank, I'd keep the dies deep in that big vault until I was ready to use them."

"You weren't joking? He does really own the bank?"

"And about half the town. Why don't you set up a watch on Ronson? When the big push comes with the dies, it's my bet he'll be right in the middle of it. Sanderson doesn't look like the kind of gent who would do much of his own gun work."

The army man agreed. "Yeah, and we can check on Sanderson at the same time."

Jim swung up to his saddle and checked the supplies. Everything was ready. Frank mounted too.

"While you're watching the saloon, take care of Melinda, the cute blonde. She can get in more trouble, pound for pound, than any ordinary human I've ever seen. Worse than a maverick coyote in a chicken coop."

"You can find the mines, Steel?"

"Yep, up the Auburn."

Jim suddenly held up his hand in a "stop" and "silence" hand signal from his army days. Jim pointed to a man climbing up the alley of a building they had just passed. He was carrying a pair of gallon cans tied together over his shoulder.

When he got to the top of the building, he opened the cans and began spreading the fluid on the roof.

"Kerosene," Jim said softly. Both men drew guns. As soon as they saw the flare of a stinker, both men fired. The arsonist gasped in surprise as one of the bullets slammed into his shoulder. The wad of sulphur matches flew from his hand. He turned and brought up his own gun just as Jim's second bullet smashed into his forehead, blasting him backwards off the roof.

As the man fell, Jim and Captain Davis spurred their horses forward down the street away from the death scene. Jim realized there probably was more than one man involved in the burning attempt. Jim waved as he turned and headed north out of town. He had a long ride ahead of him, and if possible he wanted to have one of the mines spotted before daybreak. As he rode he realized his chest didn't hurt as much today. And when he drew he hardly noticed the pull of pain.

Jim awoke in a pile of pine boughs he had cut about the time the Big Dipper told him it was two A.M. Now it was morning and he had slept well. The burning of the slices on his chest came back to torture him. The jolting ride had broken loose some of the healing that had begun.

He looked down the three hundred yards of pine-covered slope to the ravine in front of him. There was a good-sized stream, the middle fork of the American, a strange assortment of buildings, a big tunnel dug into the mountain with rail tracks, and a small stamp mill. He could see smoke starting to come from the chimney of what must be the cook shack. The sun had been up about ten minutes.

One larger building near the creek caught his eye. It was newer than the rest, built of raw lumber, and situated in an area that must have been avoided before because the creek overflowed there in winter, swamping the site. But it was dry, and the structure had a smokestack spouting a blue cloud.

A log bunkhouselike building to the left erupted with half a dozen men in various stages of dress as they headed for breakfast.

Jim had two hard biscuits and some beef jerky for his meal, washed down with stale water from his canteen. He studied the layout again.

He was here because the newspaper story

136

said this was the largest mine in the county, and it was the nearest one to town. Heavy timber came down to within ten feet of the cookshack. Jim guessed there would be a long eating table in one end and cooking gear in the other. He had to get closer.

He began by going from big tree to tree, but as he worked down the incline, the large pines disappeared, so he had to drop to his knees, working carefully from one clump of brush to the next. Jim stopped. He was coming up blind. Where he needed to be was on the other side of the shack or higher and more to the left. He retraced his route, and when in heavy timber trotted a quarter of a mile upstream, crossed over, and began working back down.

He hadn't been expecting anyone; that was part of it. Neither was he taking his usual precautions. It was his own fault, Jim realized, as he came around a big pine tree and stared at a miner who had just eased off his haunches, a cocked six-gun aimed at Jim's chest.

"Well, well, well, a visitor done tried to come in the back door," the small man facing him said. He was bearded, dirty, and wore only a pair of overalls with no shirt. Half his teeth were missing and his right eye pulled downward from an old hurt. But the important part of him was tensing on the hogsleg trigger.

Jim threw on his Southern accent and hoped. "Wal, howdy there, friend. I'm ahuntin' the Little Rock mine. Would be obliged if you-all could he'p me."

The other man eased off the trigger, a flicker of amusement showing in the gunman's eyes. "Well now, a country boy from down South. I do declare." Then his attitude changed. "What the hell you doing on Big Stake land, boy?"

"Folks in town told me you was hiring at the Little Rock mine, and I thought . . ."

"Town is nigh on to the opposite direction."

"Yeah, well, kinder got myself plumb turned around in all these blamed mountains. Where I come from a body can see nigh on to twenty mile, no trouble."

The little man with the gun hesitated. "You shore are a case. I get you dead to rights and you pull some damned story on me." He spat. "Hell, rather just shoot your ass right here like the boss said to do, but reckon I'd better take you in. They is a hand short, so they say. Keep your paws easy and take that iron out and lay it on the ground. Looks like a good piece."

Jim did as he was told. As he did, he

unsnapped the flap holding his belt knife.

They began walking along a faint trail toward the mine. Almost at once Jim fell purposely over a vine on the trail. He was trying to catch the man off guard. But the small face only laughed and waited for Jim to get up. The third time Jim stumbled and fell, the man with the gun came up and started to kick Jim. It was what Steel had been waiting for. Jim's knife came out of the sheath and slashed across the guard's thigh, bringing a gush of blood and a startled scream of pain.

Jim twisted, jumped up, and drove the blade forward. The small man clawed for his gun, but he was too late. The sharp blade drove between two ribs, into the chest cavity, and all the way through the man's heart before it stopped. He slumped to the ground as blood poured from his mouth. His eyes turned to glass and he stared up unblinking at the bright California sun.

Jim stared at the body for a moment, then grabbed its boots and pulled it to some thick brush. He was tempted to take both the six-guns, but that could be dangerous. Someone might recognize the guard's piece. At last he took his own six-gun, pulled the knife from the body, wiped it clean on the dead man's pants, and put it away.

He was more careful after that. He moved and watched, waited and then moved again. Now he was in a position to look directly into the end of the big building.

As he thought about the guard, he decided there must be more of them. But why so many gun-happy guards around a low-output mine? He must be getting close to some kind of paydirt.

Jim concentrated on the big building. It had a large metal-working machine of some kind installed there. Two men were busy at the foundations trying to level it or bolt it down to a concrete base he could see through the big door.

He saw a furnace toward the other end and a dozen more men working around the area inside and outside. The near end of the structure opened like a hayloft barn door so hay could be pulled inside. The other end of the building had a similar top door. Jim decided it might be for cooling. There would be a lot of heat if the place were used for melting down and mixing the metals needed.

But he was too far away to hear anything.

Carefully he worked his way forward, crawling from bush to bush. He was almost to the point where he could hear the workmen talking when a small sound behind him made him turn.

A guard dropped from the low branches of a tree, and before Jim could move a rifle stock slammed into the side of his head. The last thing he remembered before he slipped into unconsciousness was something about a kid's game. Everyone had agreed that it was unfair to hide in trees.

CHAPTER ELEVEN

The same night that Jim had talked to Ruth Wentz and Captain Davis at the newspaper office, Melinda eyed the customers at the Double Eagle Saloon. It was Tuesday night and the girls said this would be a slow night. They didn't know why.

Melinda looked at the huge, dirty miner who had just bought another round of drinks for their table of five. He was stupid, crude, vulgar, and out to spend his week's pay as fast as he could. She would rather have been over at the card tables making a bundle of money. Instead, she smiled and leaned toward him so he could see farther down the sharp cleavage between her breasts.

"Think you could fill that up with double eagles?" she asked him, her voice rising into a tease.

"Hell, no, but I got something else I could slide right down there." He leered at her for a moment, then reached into his pocket and took out a dollar gold piece, which he dropped into her loose bodice. She squirmed and laughed as the men expected her to. He tried to grab her, so Melinda hit his throat with the side of her hand just hard enough to hurt but not hard enough to do any damage.

"You want to get naughty, you go on upstairs. I'm busy all night." He looked disappointed as she edged away from him. As usual, he'd forgotten all about the dollar. Melinda enjoyed conning that kind of man. His brains were all in his crotch. She could lead his kind right up to the point of great expectations, then turn them down cold.

But under Melinda's smile she was becoming concerned. She hadn't heard from Jim all day. He could be anywhere. He could be bleeding or dead beside some trail.

She'd heard about his arrest and how he got away. It had been a setup, she gathered from listening to the barroom gossip. Bert Ronson had stormed into the saloon after it was over in a furious and sullen mood. He began pushing patrons around, challenging anyone in the room to draw on him. Then he picked a fight with a farmer who hadn't bothered to look up. The sheriff stepped in and stopped the one-sided brawl just before Ronson would have killed the sodbuster.

Bert drank for an hour, then moved to a poker table and began playing badly at poker.

As she thought about it, Melinda moved to another table and brought beers to four men, but kept moving. There had to be something she could do to help Jim, but what? She noticed that Bert had sobered up enough to get back his good card sense. He held most of the chips on the table in front of him. He was good at poker, and from some hands he had been called on, seemed to be an excellent bluffer.

She returned a strand of hair to the top of her head and pinned it. She liked her hair up this way, and if Bert recognized her as the girl with Jim in the hotel room, that was just too bad.

Melinda walked to the table where Bert was playing. It was a five-handed game. His beer mug was empty. She went to the bar and brought him another without his asking. He glanced up, grunted, and kept his cards closed in his big right hand.

"Yeah, lard-ass, I see your bet," Ronson growled. "I meet that and raise you thirty dollars."

The men at the table were suddenly quiet.

There was a twenty-dollar limit on bets, and it had just been enforced the hand before by Ronson. The only other player still in the pot looked at his good-sized stack of greenbacks and gold coins. He was a fat man with sagging jowels.

"We have a twenty-dollar limit," the fat man said.

"The bet is thirty dollars. Call me, you sonofabitch, or fold!" The threat came out more as a roar than a demand.

The man across the table had plenty of money to cover the bet. He looked at the other men, shrugged, and put in his thirty.

"Call," he said.

"Stupid drummer," Ronson crowed. He laid down three nines.

The man across from him coughed. "Very nice hand, but not good enough. Three jacks."

For a moment every man at the table tensed. Ronson jolted to his feet, skidding his chair backwards. His right hand whipped down to his six-gun, adjusting it, then came up to his belt. He picked up his stack of chips and money from the table and pocketed it.

The salesman from San Francisco pretended not to notice. He pulled the pot to his side, picked up the cards and shuffled them once, then held them out to Ronson.

"If you're still in the game, you've won the deal," the salesman said, straightfaced, but a crooked smile tainted it at the last moment.

Ronson's good right hand caught the round table edge and slammed it forward, tilting it against the two men on the far side, including the drummer, and toppled both of them backwards; then Ronson slammed the table over on top of them.

Bert laughed, slapping his thighs with his hands until Melinda wondered if he were having a fit. At last he stopped, picked up five double eagles from the floor, and stepped on a hand that reached for another one. He grabbed Melinda, who still stood nearby, pulled her to another table, and pointed to a chair. She sat.

His face was flushed as he stared at her across the small table. "Maybe you've noticed, honey, I don't like to lose. You're the new one, right? So far I've missed too many times with you. But tonight I'm not losing."

"Mr. Sanderson said that I didn't . . ."

He caught her face with his hand and pinched her jaws apart, stopping her speech. His hand hurt like needles.

"I don't give a damn what Mr. Sanderson

told you. I don't like to lose to him either."

He let go of her face slowly; the pain persisted. She blinked back a sudden tear.

"You want some whiskey?" she asked.

"Hell, yes. Bring a bottle and one glass."

At the bar she told the apron what she wanted and got it. She made her plans quickly. She would try to get Ronson drunk and talking. She had plenty of time, as it was only a little after eight. If that didn't work, she'd take the next most reasonable action.

She worked her plan. By ten-thirty Bert had told her about his younger days on a ranch in Montana and how his dad kicked him off the spread when he got a neighbor girl pregnant. He was eighteen at the time. She heard his story of wandering and kept pouring more whiskey into him. But he never said a word about Sanderson or his work here. She tried to probe.

"Bert, what about Sanderson? How do you fit in with his town operation? You're a ranch man."

He belched, took a long pull of the whiskey from the bottle, and grinned.

"Hell, I do lots for old Prowl. I steered him into plenty good deals. He don't mind paying right well. Got me a stack o' cash in his bank you wouldn't believe. Bertha didn't know that."

"Enough to make it worth my while?" she asked softly.

"Huh? What'n hell you say?"

"I said why don't we go up to your room and talk some more about money?"

Ronson blinked. He put his hand down to steady himself and sniffed. "You really say that?"

"Sure, the boss says I have to be extra nice to the help around here. You just got a sample the other night."

He lurched to his feet, made a stab for the bottle but missed it.

"I'll bring it," Melinda said, grabbing the whiskey.

Melinda's room was closer so she turned in there. He seemed almost out on his feet. She wondered if she'd waited too long to bring him upstairs. From experience she knew Bert was too drunk to go to bed with her. She got him into the room and let him sit on the bed before she locked the door and pulled the window shade. She lit the lamp and set it on the dresser. Her room was on the second floor but towards the back where the porch flared under her window. She had hoped that first night that Jim would come into her room that way, but he didn't.

As she looked at Bert she realized what a big man he was. With a twinge of regret she changed her battle plan again. Now all she had to do was get him to talking and ask him every question she could think of. He wouldn't remember a thing about it in the morning. When she offered him another drink he slapped it to the floor, smashing the glass.

His eyes looked better, and when he reached for her, his hand nailed her wrist like he hadn't had a drop.

"Just what the hell is your game, little bitch? You play prissy and hard to get, then suddenly you invite me up like it's my birthday. I still like you better naked like you were the other time."

For a moment panic hit and her eyes flared, her heart raced. Then she calmed. She could bluff a worse hand than this one through and win.

"Bert, you know my game; it's to pay back that fifty dollars so I can get out of this hell hole. When I'm working I encourage hard-cases like you to drink all you can. That's what I get paid for."

"Yeah, but you asked questions about Prowl. He's gonna be damned mad when I tell him."

She shrugged. "That's a damn shame.

Hell, a girl's got to talk about something while you lushes are swilling down the rot-gut whiskey."

Suddenly his attitude changed. He chuckled. "Yeah, I guess you could be right." He looked at her and grinned. "You know, big tits, you and me are a lot alike. You can be hard as a tenpenny nail. I've seen you put down some of the towners. Then you can smile sweet and go all soft and lovely."

He pulled her against him and kissed her hard, his teeth nibbling at her lips.

She submitted, deciding that he must have shaved and had a bath. Should she fight him, or should she give right in? Her gambler's mind spun through the odds and came up with her new plan. Just a little resistance, just enough to make him want her all the more. Then when he was sleeping . . .

She pushed away from him. "Bert, have you ever had a woman who really wanted you? Or do you always just move in and take what you want?"

"Don't make no damn difference. She always ends up liking it before I'm through." His hand came out and touched her breasts, then slid down the loose top of her dress.

She took a sudden breath when his hand touched her bare skin. She looked up at him defiantly. "Twenty dollars," she said firmly.

"What? You're part of my deal with Prowl."

"Your deal isn't with me. Twenty dollars is the price."

"You bitch!" He pulled his hand away from her and used it to cuff the side of her head, spilling her onto the bed. "You over-priced whore. I've never paid more than three dollars in my life."

"Then you sure go to shitty whorehouses."

Bert's surprise was followed by a blast of genuine laughter. A tear formed in one eye and he brushed it aside with his left hand.

"Woman, you are really my kind of gal." His hand caught the front of her dancehall dress. "You want me to rip this off you, or you gonna strip like a good little whore?"

She held out her hand, palm up, scowling at him.

He laughed again in grudging admiration and dropped a double eagle in her hand. She stood and went to the dresser where she scratched the coin hard. It showed gold all the way down.

An amused little thrill shot through Melinda. It was the first time she'd ever made any money this way. Did that mean she was a real whore? She wanted to giggle. She'd thrown back lot of money. She decided she

couldn't have earned the title of a professional yet; this was only part of her grand
plan, a con game to outdo anything in her
life. The money was simply part of the bait
in the trap.

She put the good double eagle on the
dresser and opened buttons and snaps, then
stepped out of her clothes until she was
naked.

"My god! Now there is a real fine
woman!" Bert said with satisfaction.

"You paid your money, man, enjoy."

It was a little after two in the morning by
her pendant watch on the dresser when
Melinda woke up. The party had lasted until
well after midnight, and the whiskey bottle
was dry. Bert had been falling-down drunk
before he at last passed out. She had found
out absolutely nothing from him about the
counterfeiting operation. She was furious,
but had plenty of time to work out exactly
what she was going to do. Bert had produced no help, so she would do the next
best thing.

Quickly she put on her undergarments
and one of her own dresses and finished
packing her suitcase. She took out the rope
she used to tie together her battered suitcase
and cut the line into four pieces. Expertly

152

she tied the big man's hands to the iron headboard of the bed. He had turned over on his back, which was exactly the way she wanted him. He groaned and started to roll over, then relaxed. As fast as she could, Melinda tied both ankles to the iron foot of the bed and stepped back.

She looked at the big Bowie knife she had taken from his belt, then at his naked body spread-eagled on the bed. The blade was razor sharp on both sides and over eight inches long. Melinda opened the window, turned down the lamp, then eased her suitcase out the opening to the porch roof and went back to the big knife. She looked at his trousers and with no pangs of conscience went through the pockets. He had ten double eagles and a stack of paper bills. She took it all and put it in her purse, which she lay beside the window.

At last she was ready. She had listened in horror as Jim told her how he had been slashed by Ronson. Now she knew the way she could help Jim was to give Ronson back some of the same pain and suffering.

She shivered as she poised the knife over the center of his hairy chest. She told herself it was just like cutting up a chicken the way she used to do back on the farm. She lowered the knife. At first the blade only lay on the warm flesh, then with a little pressure and a slicing downward motion she carved a furrow an eighth of an inch deep from collar bone to navel. It brought a grunt, then a scream of pain and terror from the naked man.

Quickly she lifted the blade to make another slice beside the first. It coursed down across the edge of his breast two inches from the first and this time she cut deeper, watching the blood bead in the wound, then run down after the knife. Ronson came to full consciousness with the start of the second cut. He jerked against the ropes and screeched in fury as he saw what she was doing. He surged upward against the ropes, but it only made the blade cut deeper into his chest.

"What the damned hell?" he roared.

She didn't say a word, only poised the knife over him again. He screamed at her, but the knife went down, and he shivered as it bit into skin and tissue for the third time.

A blubbering eruption of spittle and fury came from his tortured mouth. He screamed as she finished the cut and dropped the knife on the floor. The scream gave way to an uncontrolled sobbing as the millions of damaged nerve endings telegraphed their pain to his brain. Blood ran from the three slashes now; his chest had turned into a mass of blurred red as his life fluid dripped over his side and died in the sheet. Bert looked down at his chest and another spasm of agony and terror mixed with rage charged through him.

Melinda ran to the window, grabbed her purse, and climbed through onto the roof. She hurried with her suitcase to the edge of the porch roof at the farthest back corner. There she threw the suitcase the eight feet to the ground, sat on the edge of the roof with her feet hanging downward, just as she had done hundreds of times when she was a tomboy.

Before she could worry about it, she jumped, remembering to roll as she hit the ground to take up some of the force. Melinda felt the ground slam up and strike her feet, jolting her as her body crumpled before she turned toward her shoulder and rolled. She went over twice, then jumped up unhurt and looked up at the window she had left.

Bert Ronson had broken the ropes and now leaned out the opening, his six-gun in hand, shooting in the air. He scanned the street and alley the other way, ready to shoot anything that moved.

Melinda picked up her bag and purse and scooted under the porch overhang before

Ronson saw her. She walked quickly to the alley and down a block. She was running now, but she didn't have the slightest idea where she was going. Her only thought had been revenge for Jim. Now she knew she had to get as far away as she could from that ugly, bleeding chest of Bert Ronson.

Chapter Twelve

As she ran along the alley, Melinda tried furiously to decide where she could go. She knew no one in town. Bert would try to come after her, and Prowl Sanderson would hear about it quickly. Where could she hide?

From one of her overheard conversations she remembered Ronson bad-talking the local newspaper. The paper had accused Prowl of not doing what was right for the good of the town. Then she remembered Jim said he was going to stop by the paper to do some research. It might be a place she could find a friend.

But as she ran down the rest of the long alley, her skirt trapping her legs into short steps and the suitcase banging against her legs, she realized she didn't know the location of the newspaper office.

When she came to California Street again she paused in the shadows. No one walked the street this time of night for her to ask. She couldn't go to the sheriff because he would take her right back to the Double Eagle Saloon. She tried to think, then remembered one morning when she had taken a short walk. She had passed the office of the *Clarion.* It was on California Street, too, and couldn't be far away. She spotted the big sign on the Double Eagle Saloon and turned, walking away from it.

Suddenly she remembered that she hadn't taken off her dancehall makeup. Her rouged cheeks, painted lips, and made-up eyes branded her at once as a dancehall girl. No respectable woman in town would speak to her. At least there would be men at the newspaper office. Yes, this was the right way. She looked from door to door until she got her bearings. The office she wanted was half a block down.

Gratefully she walked now instead of running. At the office door she paused, just a second, then knocked hard. The windows were all dark. She waited, then banged against the door with her foot and listened but could hear nothing.

Melinda scowled as she glanced up the street and saw a deputy sheriff walking in the other direction. Soon he would be coming down this side of the block. She looked at the door again. It had small glass panes in it. She used the corner of her suitcase and broke the pane nearest to the door handle. Melinda reached inside carefully and turned the skeleton key she found in the lock, then opened the door and stepped inside. It wasn't the first place she had broken into.

The room was black. Nothing moved or made a sound. She closed the door quietly, locked it again, and put the key on the floor. Then, when her eyes became more accustomed to the darkness, she moved around the long counter and found a chair to sit in. She wanted to take off her shoes and relax, but she didn't. The chair was at a desk, so she leaned forward and laid her head down on her arms. It would be easy to go to sleep in almost any position right then, she decided.

Suddenly the door into the back room burst open.

"Don't move!" a man's voice instructed. "This is a shotgun and it'll blow you in half."

Melinda sat very still.

A moment later a lamp held high so it wouldn't blind the carrier came through the door from the back shop. She saw the glint of light off the barrel of the weapon.

"Fer catfish, you all alone?" the man asked.

"Yes, can you help me?"

"You from one of the saloons?"

She nodded. He put the lamp down on the table.

"It's happened before," he said. "I'm Wentz, Barney Wentz. Come on upstairs and I'll turn you over to my daughter, Ruth. She's got a good shoulder, case you want to do some bawling." The man became silent. He was about fifty, with gray hair, a friendly face, and a short, wiry body. His hands were still smudged with ink and grease.

Melinda smiled at him and for the first time in an hour, she felt safe. "Thanks, I . . . I didn't know where else to go."

The man was squinting at her. "You hurt, Miss? Got some blood on your sleeve there."

"No, no, I'm not hurt."

He lifted his brows, rubbed an itch on his nose that demanded immediate attention, and turned, picking up the lamp.

"Well, come on this way; Ruth will help you no matter what your trouble is."

She followed him through the door into the back shop section of the newspaper office. She saw snatches of machines, a low row of cabinets that she decided held type. A press of some sort sat in a place of

160

importance across from a big slab of marble.

After walking up some stairs, they came to the living quarters. A girl with long brown hair and a small, upturned nose came through a door.

"Trouble?" she asked, looking at her father.

" 'Pears as how," he said, turned, and went into the farthest room and closed the door.

It gave the women a short time to size each other up. Melinda saw a girl about her own age in a loose, inexpensive blue flannel nightgown with long sleeves, gathered at the throat with a blue ribbon. Melinda liked her at once.

"A problem?" Ruth asked.

Melinda suddenly felt very harsh, brazen, and definitely outclassed by this softly feminine creature. She nodded.

"May I call you Ruth? I'm Melinda."

They stared at each other for a moment, then both smiled.

"Sit down over here, Melinda, and tell me all about it."

They moved to the daybed and sat, then quickly Melinda explained how she had to work in the saloon to pay off her debt. She told how she was also trying to find out something about the missing gold dies for Jim Steel.

Melinda watched Ruth as she heard Jim's name. Ruth looked up quickly, eyes pinched just a little, her mouth opened in surprise.

Ruth regained her composure almost at once and picked at some lint on her nightgown. "And have you known Mr. Steel very long?"

"Oh, two or three years. We're just good friends. I run into him now and then. We happened to see each other in Virginia City and when I found out he was coming here, I told him I was, too. It was the longest stage ride in history, so rough and hot."

As soon as she said it, Melinda realized that it sounded like a lie, but it was the truth.

Ruth told Melinda about the talk she had with Jim earlier that evening and that he was going out to check on two gold mines in the back country.

"Thank goodness," Melinda said. "I thought he might be getting himself into trouble again."

Ruth watched the other woman with a strange new feeling. Was she jealous of this painted female? Melinda did seem to be a strong person, determined, not afraid to battle with men in a man's world of gambling. For that Ruth admired her. But to serve drinks at a saloon . . . She knew they both should be going to bed, but the blonde woman was interesting and likeable. She couldn't resist one last probe. "Melinda, you do like this Jim Steel a lot, don't you?"

Melinda felt herself start to blush, then by will power alone she stopped it. She blinked, then looked steadily at Ruth.

"Yes, Jim Steel is a very special kind of man. Any girl who could marry him would be very lucky."

That was when Ruth knew intuitively that Melinda was not only a professional woman gambler; she had slept with Jim as well, probably many times. Melinda would marry him if she could. She had already possessed the man in whom Ruth slowly realized that she was more than casually interested. In fact, she was so fascinated by him that she had not even considered slapping his face when he kissed her. She admitted to herself that she had not backed away. In fact, she had been the one to lean forward until her breasts brushed his chest, thrilling her. She had been thankful when he had turned to leave. Oh, yes, she had wanted him. She had wanted him more than any man she had ever met.

Now Ruth looked back at Melinda. This woman was gross and simple and straight-forward. She probably undressed first for

Jim. She went after what she wanted. Ruth sighed, knowing that she could never do anything like that. Oh, she could go out and track down a good news story. But she would always be a lady rather than stoop to anything common just to win a man. The more Melinda talked, the more Ruth realized what the girl was. She could find only one phrase for it, *a common whore.*

Melinda had tried to figure out Ruth Wentz from the first moment she met her. She was a "lady"; that was certain, and from what she had said, Melinda knew very well that Ruth was just as interested in Jim Steel as she was, even though she had met him briefly only twice. Yes, he was special, Melinda knew, and if he could excite a cold, calculating woman like Ruth, he must be much better than she realized.

But as Melinda evaluated Ruth, she came up with a simple term to describe her . . . *a conceited snob.*

They soon decided it was too early to stay up and too late not to get some more sleep. Ruth made up a bed for Melinda on the daybed.

"Now, don't worry about Prowl Sanderson," Ruth said. "He doesn't scare me at all. We'll protect you here for just as long as you want to stay, and in the meantime, we

164

can both see how we can help Jim find those dies."

Melinda smiled. "Thanks, Ruth. I didn't know where to go. And thanks for telling me about Jim. I was sure he was going to fool around and get himself into trouble again."

CHAPTER THIRTEEN

Jim Steel groaned and fought down another wave of pain. He realized he was in some large river, maybe going over a falls or through rapids. More water sloshed in his face and he gasped, then the pain drilled into his side again and he couldn't figure it out. Maybe he had hit a big rock in the rapids. The pains came then from all angles, on his legs, his back, his stomach. He flailed out with his hands as his head went under water again and something smashed into his chest. He screamed.

Jim sat up and found himself not in a river. Another bucketful of water splashed into his face and a moan seeped from between tightly clenched teeth. Now he was fully conscious. He sat on the ground in the center of the Big Stake mining camp. Six men stood around him, staring down. One had an axe handle, another a spade, a third a long stick, and they all wore heavy boots and knew how to use them. He turned one way and a boot thudded into his side.

"RRRRRRRRRAAAAAAAAAUUUUU-UUGGGGGGGGHHHHHHHHHH!" The scream ripped from Jim's throat.

"Well, now, we caught a crybaby," a voice in back of him said. Jim turned his head to see who was talking, and as he did, another boot drove into his stomach, doubling him over. Waves of pain and nausea billowed through him. He fought it back, pushed down the blinding blackness, and pulled himself up to a sitting position.

"What the hell's your name, buddy?" The voice, strong and demanding, came from in front of him. Jim blinked twice to clear water from his eyes, then focused on the rough-looking miner in jeans and plaid lumberjack's shirt. He wore a six-inch full heard.

Jim started to stand, but never made it. A foot came out, a hand pushed and he tripped and crumpled, rolling over twice in the dust.

When Jim sat up this time, he could talk. "Looking for work," he said.

"Hell he was!" another voice countered. "Sneaking down here from upstream like some damn rebel spy. I've seen enough to know. Belly-crawling through the woods. He warn't lookin' for no job."

The bearded man grabbed Jim's shirt front and pulled him erect with one hand. Again the gushing of pain pushed him close to unconsciousness. But he held on.

"What'n hell you looking for, Mister?"

As the man spoke he saw a red stain seeping through Jim's shirt. The man motioned and two miners came forward and held Jim as the bearded one unbuttoned Jim's shirt and opened it. They saw the bandages then, the caked, dried blood almost covered with a surge of fresh red soaking into the wrappings around his chest and stomach.

"My god, he's been sliced up; put him down."

They stood back as Jim was spread out on the ground.

"Now, Mister, I don't hold with torturing a man. If you're from the Little Rock mine you just nod. I got no stomach for watchin' a man die." He turned. "Hey, bring the man a drink of water."

They watched as he pushed up on elbows to drink from the long-handled tin dipper. Jim took the water eagerly. He glanced down at his red chest. It looked like many of the healed places had been torn open again. He tried to speak, hoping he could trust his voice.

"Ain't this the Little Rock? Supposed to be there. Somebody said they was hirin'."

The bearded man spat into the dust. "You done missed it by near two gullies." He frowned and shrugged. "What the hell, we got work to do here or we'll get our asses burned. You go back down there half a mile, then up the next little trail. It's over in there to hell and gone."

Jim got to his knees, then two men lifted him to his feet.

"You gonna make it?" someone asked.

Jim waved.

"Just don't go and die on our goddamn claim," another voice called.

Jim looked around to get his bearings, then spotted the slope where he left Hamlet and began shuffling in that direction. He had no idea how many times he had been kicked or hit with the sticks, but his chest felt like one big, blood-wet wound. At first it took exacting concentration to keep moving one foot ahead of the other. It was like learning to walk again. He had to think through every move. He couldn't have lost that much blood.

Slowly he worked toward the slope, and when he started to climb, it took every ounce of his strength to move up the hill.

169

As soon as he entered the fringes of the woods and they couldn't see him from the mine, he leaned against a pine tree to rest. He knew if he sat down he'd never get up. For five minutes he held onto the tree; then he felt his knees caving in. Slowly he slid down the trunk, sprawling on his back in the soft, fresh grass.

When Jim awoke, he was still on his back. One hand over his face swatted unconsciously at flies which had swarmed around the ripe blood scent. The fading sun shone from behind trees in the west. He had no idea how long he had been sleeping, but there couldn't be more than an hour until sunset. He moved so he could see his chest. Most of the blood had dried, which had to mean the new bleeding had stopped. Jim tried to sit up and found he could do so with comparative ease. He felt ten times as good as he had before he slid down the pine tree. Slowly he pushed up to his knees and felt only a few familiar twinges in his chest. He reached for the rough bark of the Jeffery pine, glad for the convenient handholds.

A gasp of pain stabbed through him as he pulled himself to his feet. He waited for the shock of the pain to wear itself out; then he thought about Hamlet. The big buckskin would not wander far.

It took Jim half an hour to find the horse. He had grazed up the slope, feeding on tasty shoots of grass. Finding the ex-actor horse was only the first problem. How in hell was he going to mount him? There was no convenient downed tree he could use as a step. Hamlet wasn't a trick horse who could lie down beside him, let him fall into the saddle, and then stand up. A normal mounting would mean a pull on his stomach muscles that would be so brutal he would probably pass out again.

He practiced lifting his foot, and after three tries got it into the stirrup. He held to the saddle for support, dreading the thought of swinging his other foot over the horse. He tried twice but couldn't stand up in the stirrup. Each time waves of pain shattered him, bringing beads of sweat to his forehead. The third time he decided he had to do it. He closed his eyes and surged upward, putting all of his energy into standing in the first stirrup. A cry like that of a tortured animal spewed from his lips as the stomach muscles reacted to the sudden pull. He fell into the saddle, surging forward so he had to catch himself against the beast's broad neck.

Jim lay against the mane, sucking in air. A

dozen lungfuls came and went before he dared open his eyes. He held his legs still and gasped again as a final spasm of pain rocketed up and down his red chest, then faded.

Five minutes later he urged the buckskin to move. At first each step was like a whip-saw of pain. Jim reached down deeply and came up with a new reserve of strength, gripped the reins, and turned Hamlet toward Sacramento. He thought about Melinda, about Ruth, about the mine. Anything but the jolting discord of pain that came from his chest like an out-of-tune symphony orchestra.

From what he had seen at the mine, there was plenty of equipment, power, and space as well as manpower for a counterfeiting operation. And the double set of roving and fixed guards meant it was more than just a non-productive mine. That had a touch of the professional about it. Jim was sure that Bert Ronson had set up the security system.

The big stamping press seemed to be in the process of installation, which meant they were not quite ready. Or perhaps they had moved it or adjusted it. Maybe by tomorrow. Jim settled down to the long, slow ride back to town, sure that he had found the right spot. Only now what the hell could he do about it?

It was well past dark when Jim rode into Sacramento by the same slow but safe route he had used before. He must still be a wanted man in this little town, and he had no wish to be spotted by a gun-happy deputy. Gun? It was the first time he had thought about his six-gun. But when he reached down he found it still in the holster. Someone at the mine must have pushed it back into his holster as he stood up.

He made it to the alley unnoticed and walked Hamlet close to the back door of the *Clarion* office. There was little chance anyone would see his horse here or that it would be recognized as belonging to Jim. About half the houses still had lights on. The saloons were just getting warmed up for a night of beer, cards, and brawling.

First he had to get down from Hamlet. He spotted a pair of heavy wooden crates and rode to them, swung off, and in one tortuous movement was on the boxes, then on the ground. He leaned against the horse until the darting pains ran their course, then tied Hamlet and went to the *Clarion* door.

It took four hard poundings before anyone came. At last he saw a light moving toward the door from inside.

"Who is it?"

"Jim," he said.

The door opened at once and he went inside. Ruth caught his shoulders and held him as he sagged.

"Oh, dear god, Jim, you're hurt!" She called for her father and between them they got him up the stairs and to the daybed. When he opened his eyes again he saw Melinda.

"Hey, we've been worried about you."

He grimaced and lay back on the softness. "Suppose I could bother one of you ladies for some whiskey?"

Melinda brought it. Ruth came back with scissors and a sheet. Jim drank. As Ruth began cutting away the bloody bandages and soaking them off, Melinda tore the sheet into strips. Even though Ruth was careful and had a delicate touch, the removal of the old dressing was a new torture. Half the cloth had glued itself to the wound with dried blood. It took more soaking.

A half hour later the old bandages were gone. Ruth rested while Melinda washed off the caked blood and got his torso cleaned up for the new dressing. They had no ointment to put on the wounds. Jim refused to go to the doctor or to call him there.

As they worked he told them a little of

what had happened and how he was sure he had found the location where the new double eagles would be counterfeited.

Ruth's father came upstairs after putting in sixteen hours in the shop below and fell into a chair. He watched the women working on Jim. Jim handed the bottle to Wentz and he took a straight shot.

Neither man said a word. They took turns drinking slugs of the whiskey. At last Barney Wentz nodded to Ruth.

"He's ready for the wrapping now."

The whiskey had dulled his whole body, and the pains that came through as the women wrapped his chest and stomach were only dull aches. Twice he shivered and moaned until they eased the pressure on a bandage. The next time he looked, they were finished. Melinda wiped his sweating forehead with a damp cloth.

"Now, we're going to keep you right there in bed for at least two days, just like the doctor told you."

"She's right," Ruth said. "You need rest and time to let the healing start again. I'm afraid you're going to have some scars before this is all over."

She sat beside him. "Anyway, tomorrow the story comes out in the *Clarion* about the missing dies and the counterfeiting."

Jim tried to sit up. "What?"

"My story comes out in the paper tomorrow; it's Thursday, our publication day. I had a letter from San Francisco that tells a lot more about the dies. And I don't know if you're going to like this or not, but the government has reward posters for the dies. A thousand dollars!"

Jim hit the bed with the flat of his hand and swore; a round dozen choice phrases blurted from his mouth before he scowled at the women.

Melinda laughed.

Ruth lifted her brows in surprise. "Oh, don't stop just because of me. I've heard worse talk."

"I was just getting warmed up," Jim said. "Why the hell did they put out a reward? Now we'll have bounty hunters by the dozen swarming in here in two days. Damn!"

Barney Wentz reached an ink-stained hand for the whiskey bottle. "It sure ain't gonna help you none, son. Think you know where the work is gonna take place?"

"Got to be at the Big Stake mine."

"We'll worry about that in the morning," Ruth said, picking up the lamp. "Right now it's time we all got some sleep. Melinda, I've got plenty of space in my room."

Melinda smiled. "You don't think that I should sleep here on the daybed? I did last night."

Ruth blushed. "No, I don't think so, Melinda." She turned and went into her bedroom. As Mr. Wentz moved to the other lamp, Melinda bent and kissed Jim's lips, then jumped back.

"I'll see you tomorrow," Jim said, then settled down on the softness of the daybed and let the exhaustion and pains in his chest sweep up and over him. He was sleeping within two minutes.

The heavy smell of cooking bacon woke Jim the next morning. There were eggs, oatmeal, toast and coffee and wild plum jam. Jim knew he was in heaven. He hadn't smelled food that good since he left Virginia City. He started to roll over, stopped, and sat up instead. The chest pains were receding again. He swung his feet off the daybed and put on his boots, then his new shirt, now as bloody as his old one.

Ruth came in from the kitchen and shook her head. "That won't do at all. Let me see if one of Dad's shirts will fit."

It didn't. As soon as the mercantile opened, she went over and bought him a new shirt, plain blue, that reminded Jim of the kind the men wore in Nevada State Prison.

He was eager to get out on the street, but he couldn't afford to run into the sheriff.

"Why not wear a disguise?" Melinda asked. "A big hat and some old clothes and a cane. Be an old man all hunched over." Melinda had washed off her saloon makeup and Jim liked her better without it.

After breakfast was over he found an old hat and Ruth gave him a baggy sweater someone had left in the office. Ruth got a cane and he practiced tottering around the room, to the amusement of both women. The first big test was getting down the steps. As Melinda helped him, she had her arm around his shoulders and she didn't mind the work at all.

Downstairs he walked out the front door of the *Clarion,* and the first thing he saw was a boy tacking a poster on the building next door. He read it:

"REWARD, $1,000.00. For information leading to the recovery of the dies for the 1867 Gold Double Eagle coins. These dies are opposed pieces of metal, concave in appearance and of no value to anyone else, but important to the U.S. Treasury Department."

Jim turned away from it and headed up

the street at a slow, shuffling pace, one hand planted firmly on the cane. But his eyes were moving faster, drinking in anything they could see. Posters about the reward decorated every fourth building along the street.

There were copies of the *Clarion* stacked in the mercantile, hardware, and half the other stores. The drifters and bounty hunters would be close behind. Already he saw more men wearing guns on the street than he had two days ago.

Quick, easy money was a magnet that drew most men. And Jim was well aware that a thousand dollars was four years' pay for the hard work of a cowhand and some miners. It was more cash than the average merchant in town took in all year. The place would be crawling with bounty hunters within a week.

He crossed the street slowly, kicking up a cloud of the soft, powdery dust. When he reached the boardwalk on the other side, he saw two black horses with army brands and army saddles. At the hitching rail in front of the stage office Jim stopped. He was moving better than he thought he would. His shuffle was a put-on now; he knew he would be able to walk normally if he tried. He shuffled another few steps down the boardwalk unnoticed by most of the Sacramento citizens, but he watched everything. Half a block ahead he saw two men in army blue striding toward him. One had the double bars of a cavalry captain on his shoulders. Jim waited and when the officer was two paces in front, he said:

"Captain Davis, sir."

The army man stopped, looked at Jim and twitched his moustache before moving closer. "Yes."

"I see you got your uniform. Does look a mite better than those damn civvies."

The captain frowned, looked closer. "Jim?"

"Right. Like my new suit?"

The captain grinned now. "Yeah, it is an improvement."

Jim pretended to hit him with his cane.

"Jim, I'm worried. We're going to have a hoard of reward busters in here damn soon. You know anything new?"

Jim told him quickly how he thought he had the site spotted and where it was. "You keeping tabs on Ronson?"

"Sure. He's drinking and whoring, all day and all night. Hear somebody sliced up his chest good. Must look like yours."

"Lucky guy. Keep track of him. He'll be in on any big play. Your new troops get in?"

"No, just two men on an advance party. Rest due later today."

They stopped talking as a pair of men sauntered by. Before they spoke again a fancy democrat buggy wheeled down the street in back of a prancing, pure white animal that looked more like an Eastern race pony than a quarter horse. The tall, thin man with a skeletal face never glanced at them.

"Is that Sanderson?" Jim asked.

Captain Davis nodded.

"Put a man on him and see where he goes. If he heads north out the Donner Trail, have your man hightail it back here and tell you. Leave word for me at the newspaper office."

Captain Davis flicked his hand at the sergeant who stood beside him. The man wheeled, casually got on his black army mount, and moved down the street after the fancy buggy.

Prowl Sanderson had seen the army men on the corner as he passed. A captain, which meant he would be the Captain Davis quoted in the *Clarion* story. The paper had come very close to the truth, and he had no idea where that girl writer dug up her facts. But she carefully attributed every statement to some authority, the state attorney general, or the army, or the Bureau of the Mint. He had read the article a dozen times and now had his lawyer digesting it for any way he could bring a lawsuit against the paper. He doubted if there were.

His thin face pulled even tighter over the high cheekbones. Just a few more days and it wouldn't matter what she printed. The metal stamping machine was in final position and all ready. He moved his fancy boot backwards under the buggy seat until it touched the carpetbag he had casually placed there. The bag contained the latest shipment, ten thousand dollars' worth of pure gold. Very soon now he would convert that into one hundred thousand dollars' worth of perfect counterfeit double eagles, using the government's own dies! It was a highlight in his career. He soon would be able to sell out his holdings in Sacramento and go anywhere, taking the dies along to replenish his supply of double eagles whenever he felt the need.

It had been a long struggle, but now his victory was within his grasp. He cracked the whip over the flashy white mare as they pulled out of town and headed northeast toward the American River and his Big Stake mine.

He had left strict instructions with Ronson. The man had functioned well in limited assignments. He would give him the bonus of five thousand dollars in double eagles. But then he would be through with Ronson. The man was too crude for the delicate job of distribution of counterfeit coins.

Today Ronson would take care of the newspaper office much quicker than the lawyer could. But he had carefully instructed Ronson specifically not to kill anyone. The girl and her father were to be taken out of the plant before he set fire to it. If there were no killing, the sheriff could handle it. But if both the Wentzes were dead, the damn state attorney general would step in sure as hell.

Once the *Clarion* was gone, another paper would be hard to start. Maybe he should open a paper of his own so he could have total and absolute control. Yes, if he stayed here he would do that. Hire a newspaperman and back him and make the town think he was independent.

Prowl settled back in the well-padded seat, proud to have the fanciest buggy in town with a high-stepping white mare. He never liked to show his emotion, but right now he was so excited about this last phase of three months of plans and hard work that he wanted to shout. He never shouted. But this was a special occasion. In two days he would have it done. He would be a millionaire! Prowl Sanderson said the word out loud:

"Millionaire! Millionaire! Millionaire!"

CHAPTER FOURTEEN

The instant the masked man came through the front door of the *Clarion* office Ruth reached for the pistol she kept in back of the counter. That was the one she had given to Jim Steel.

The masked man waved his own gun at her and motioned to the back room. He quickly locked the front door and hurried the frightened girl as she walked into the back shop. His shot into the ceiling brought a noisy hand-cranked press to a sudden stop as Barney looked up into the still-smoking barrel of the .44.

"Hands over your head, old man," the gruff voice demanded. As they both stood that way, the man pulled out a drawer filled with the tiny pieces of type and let them scatter over the floor. He laughed. "Damn, I always wanted to do that."

"What do you want?" Barney asked.

"Shut up, old man, and get over here."

Barney walked near him.

"Turn around and put your hands behind you." Barney did and was quickly tied. The man found a gallon can of kerosene, smelled it and grinned. He opened it and sloshed the fluid over the wooden floor, then into a box of ruined paper from the big press.

"That should make a fine little bonfire, don't you think, uppity woman?"

"If you're trying to scare us, it won't work," Ruth said. "You work for Prowl Sanderson, right?"

"Shut up, dumb bitch!"

Ruth turned away from him. If only Melinda didn't come down there was a chance they might be saved. If Melinda could shoot a gun . . . if she heard anything . . . then Ruth's hopes shattered as Melinda came halfway down the open stairs from the living quarters.

"I thought I heard a shot," she said. Then she saw the man with the mask. Melinda scampered for the back door, but the man with the gun beat her to it. He pushed her backward, then slapped her hard and laughed as she fell.

"I'll be damned, look what I caught! The little tiger who likes to play with knives."

Melinda turned, fear shadowing her pretty face. He stepped closer to her, his eyes now murderous. Her lips formed his name and just then he slapped her hard again. He gasped as his chest muscles reacted. Melinda spun backwards away from him, but he caught her wrist with his powerful left hand and held her.

"When we got outside, I want you to do exactly as I tell you." He turned, lit a single match, held it to a wad of thirty stinkers stuck together. When the whole group blazed he threw it into the kerosene-soaked papers. "Outside!"

They ran through the back door as the flames ate into the paper and quickly spread to the wooden floor and walls. Outside they found a buggy at the back door. The man with the gun bundled them aboard and whipped the horse toward the far end of the alley. In back of them smoke began to seep out the back windows and door of the Sacramento *Clarion* office.

Jim had been moving back toward the newspaper office after touring the street when he saw the man go into the *Clarion*. He was only two stores away, so he dropped his shuffle and walked quickly toward the building. As the man went inside Jim saw him pull a kerchief up into a mask. Jim stopped at the window and looked inside. The man had his gun out and was motioning to Ruth. Over the mask the man looked familiar, but Jim couldn't tie him down. Jim reacted immediately, reaching for his hogsleg before he realized he wasn't wearing it. His little disguise might turn out to be a costly mistake.

Jim looked for somebody from whom he could borrow a gun. Two men walked toward him, but neither wore a sidearm. He rushed into the mercantile three doors down. The clerk was busy with a customer.

"Hey, somebody's robbing the newspaper. Loan me a six-gun, somebody!"

The clerk looked up and scowled. "You'll have to see the owner about that."

"Where is he?"

"Ain't in yet."

Jim wanted to wring the kid's neck. He turned. "You got a door to the alley?"

The clerk pointed and Jim walked quickly toward it. He found he was moving easily, without the chest pains. He ran. He eased the back door open cautiously and looked out. He had hopes of surprising the gunman when he came through the newspaper back door or to get inside and overpower the man before he got away.

But when Jim looked out, he saw smoke coming from the office and a man with a gun pushing Melinda into a buggy. Before Jim could get outside, the rig raced down the alley.

Jim stood for a moment frozen. All of his senses were working, gathering facts, impressions, then making the decision. Hamlet stood two doors down. He surged out the door and ran, adrenalin pouring into the bloodstream. A few seconds later he was through the newspaper office door, choking on the smoke, charging up the steps to the living quarters. The fire was still confined to the front of the shop. He found his six-gun and belt hanging over the chair and grabbed it, buckling it on as he ran back down the stairs. He had to get outside in time to see which way the buggy turned.

But he didn't. When he got out the door and looked, the alley was empty. He ran for Hamlet, made one lunging try, and mounted the buckskin with almost no pain. He jerked the big horse around and pounded down the alley after the buggy. At the street he looked closely at the dust and saw the buggy had turned to the left, down Apple Street. With any luck he could track the rig all the way, right to its destination, especially if it used back streets where there was little traffic from wagons.

He looked ahead, thought he saw a buggy,

but couldn't be sure. Now he jogged along, making sure he followed the same thin set of buggy wheel tracks. They continued straight down Apple for three blocks, then the houses thinned and there were no more cross streets. Again the rig turned, this time down a narrow lane. At the end stood three houses. He pulled Hamlet to a stop. Two of the houses had buggies in front of them. He looked at them critically. One home was neat, with flowers growing in beds around a carefully trimmed yard. The house on the other side seemed abandoned, with weeds growing high in the front yard and a window broken.

Jim dismounted and walked the horse toward the house with a broken window. He came up on the side away from town, dropped Hamlet's reins, and crawled toward the front porch. Jim moved up so he could see through the glass in the door. Bert Ronson, mask down, slapped Melinda hard, driving her to her knees.

Jim wanted to burst through the door and blast Ronson with a pair of bullets through his heart, but the women were too close. Ruth stood almost behind Ronson. He had to move in slowly.

Jim put his hands on the knob and began to turn it gradually, hoping the mechanism didn't squeak. He had the door unlatched now and had begun to swing it open when he heard a scream. As the door opened, his right hand came up with the Colt. Then he saw the reason for the cry. Ronson stood beside Ruth, the front of her dress in his hands; the woman was exposed from faintly pink-tipped breasts to the brown triangle of hair at her crotch. Ruth seemed too surprised or shocked to move. She stood there staring at Ronson. Jim had no room for a shot. Before he could say a word, Melinda charged Ronson.

"Goddamn beast," she screamed, scratching and clawing at the man's face. "Beast! No good, goddamn beast!"

Ronson backed up a step in surprise, then swept Melinda aside with one massive arm and reached toward Ruth, who hadn't moved.

"Hold it, Ronson!" Jim roared, his six-gun leveled at Bert's heart. "One move, Ronson, and you're buzzard meat." Jim never took his gaze off Ronson. "Melinda, get Ruth out of there, and put some clothes over her. Slap her if you have to to bring her out of her spell."

Melinda caught Ruth's hand and pulled her to one side.

Ronson laughed. "So the shining knight

191

has come to rescue the pure maiden, is that it, Steel? Now you gonna shoot me down without no chance like you did my men?"

"Where are the gold dies, Ronson?"

"The dies? You don't want them, remember?"

"I changed my mind. Did Sanderson take them to the Big Stake mine this morning?"

"You'll never know, Steel, 'cause I draw faster than you do."

"Not in a fair fight, Ronson. Did Sanderson take those dies this morning?"

"Yeah, Steel. He's turning out double eagles by the hundreds, right now, and I'm gonna kill you and take care of this snotty bitch; then I'll go help Sanderson."

"Why should I even give you a chance to draw, Ronson?"

Bert grinned, the white scar showing even plainer. "Because you got that honest streak in you, Steel. That's what causes you all your trouble. You can't be a straight outlaw; you got to try to play both sides of the game, and this time it's gonna get you killed."

"Don't listen to that, Jim. Go ahead, shoot him. No jury in this town will convict you," Melinda said.

"Sure, Jim. Gun me down, murder me in cold blood. Hell, you're not dirty enough,

Steel. Bet you've never shot a man in the back or used a razor on one, have you? Never sliced a man's throat when he didn't even know you had a blade. Hell, no. You're soft, Steel. Soft and too damn honest."

Slowly Jim uncocked the six-gun, let the hammer down gently on the full chamber and, without looking, tapped the muzzle on the front edge of the holster. Then he gently lowered the gun into its leather home. Jim's hand dropped to his side, his fingers flexing.

"No, Jim, no!" Melinda cried.

"Now, ever' gent's got an equal chance," Ronson said. "Let's see how fast you are, sucker!"

Jim saw the other man's hand streak for his gun. Jim drove his hand downward, palm gluing to the exposed handle, fingers clawing into position, arm coming up with the weapon naturally, as if it were a part of the hand.

In those fractions of a second, which can mean the difference between life and death, Jim saw Ronson turn sideways, saw his left hand streak down toward the pistol before it was leveled and knew Ronson was going to fan the hammer with his other hand to speed the first shot.

Jim's fluid draw and his finger on the trigger had his weapon nearly half cocked before it came out of leather. The trigger was moving back to its zenith, getting ready to fall. The moment the gun muzzle stopped moving and steadied, the hammer broke over the high point and came forward toward a fresh round. Jim's hand aimed in a natural, almost automatic reflex pointing action honed to perfection by years of practice against jars and bottles and trees, and more men than he cared to remember.

Despite Jim's lightning-fast draw and firing, he heard the other man's fanned weapon fire a split second before his own. But as Jim looked out through the faint tendrils of blue smoke from his muzzle, he saw his bullet slam into Ronson's side and jolt him three feet backward. Ronson hit the wall and slid slowly down it, his left hand over his side wound. He still held the smoking revolver in his right hand, a surprised expression on his face.

"That's the problem with fanning the hammer, Ronson, you give away accuracy for time."

"Finish me," Ronson said. "You gutshot me; I don't want to die that slow. Finish me!"

"You'll live to face a whole list of federal charges," Jim said. He started to turn away.

"Look out, Jim!" Ruth screamed.

It happened so quickly Jim couldn't say if he thought through it or acted by reflex. As he spun around he saw Ronson lifting the six-gun, the hammer moving backwards. Jim hadn't holstered his weapon yet, and it went off three times, as fast as he could pull the trigger. One of the lead messengers caught Ronson in the jaw, blowing off half his face, splattering the wallpaper with blood, jaw-bone fragments, and scattered bits of flesh. The second bullet took him in the middle of the throat, shattering his Adam's apple and sending a red tide of blood gushing down his shirt front. The third slug struck the gun Ronson held, splintering lead sliv-ers into the already dead man's face and smashing the weapon from his hand.

Jim watched the figure slump toward the floor this time before he relaxed. He heard a whimper behind him and began to turn.

"No, please, don't look at me," Ruth said.

"Ruth, let's go in the next room," Melinda said calmly.

While they were gone, Jim stared at the body against the far wall. The man had asked to die, deserved to die. He'd just saved the state of California the expense of a trial and a hanging. Still it rankled him. Maybe Ronson had been right, he did have a major flaw — that damn streak of fair play that had troubled him. He opened his revolver and kicked out the spent cartridges and pushed in new ones. He eased the cylinder back in, making sure the firing pin came down on the empty chamber. His honest streak might get him into some trouble, but it sure as hell had kept him out of prison and off the gallows — so far.

When the women came back a minute later, Ruth was properly covered. Melinda had taken the torn dress and made part of it into a wrapper and the rest into a shawl. Ruth still stared straight ahead and wouldn't say a word to Jim. He got the women outside and into the buggy and Hamlet tied onto the back. Melinda pointed at the house.

"Hey, Mr. Wentz is still in there. Bert put him in another room."

When Jim found Barney Wentz he was lying on the floor, gagged and tied hand and foot. He freed him and Barney asked what the shooting was about. In the buggy Melinda went over the details of the gunfight and reminded Barney that the *Clarion* office was probably burned to the ground.

The little man sighed, looked up at Ruth, and shook his head. "Damnit. Better take us to the hotel. We'll put up there until we decide what's left we can salvage."

Fifteen minutes later, Jim and Melinda were on their way toward the Big Stake mine in the buggy borrowed from the late Bert Ronson. They went past the *Clarion* office and saw it had burned to a furious pile of twisted machinery. The bucket brigade had saved the saddle shop and hardware store on each side of it, partly because they had brick walls.

At first Jim told Melinda she wasn't going to the mine.

"I sure as hell am going," she began. "You don't think I'm going to miss out on the fun of capturing those dies, do you? I'm also going to be there to find out how much gold Mr. Sanderson has stashed out there that we're going to split fifty-fifty."

So he took her along. He had decided to as soon as she suggested it, but he liked to listen to her when she got suddenly angry. When she was through he pointed down the street, giving her the reins so she could drive.

They went by buggy as far as Jim thought they safely could, then hid it in some trees about a mile from the mine and moved ahead on foot. Melinda wasn't dressed for cross-country hiking, but she adapted. She broke shoulder straps and took off two of the fluffy petticoats and left them in the buggy. Her shoes were square-heeled and sturdy.

"Ready," she announced, and they moved toward the mine. Jim had picked out potential enemy guardpost positions as he approached. He left Melinda behind a big tree and worked up silently toward the first, a dead snag that had toppled and been blackened by a forest fire years ago. It was on a point a hundred feet over the trail and had enough knotholes and burned-out sections to make it a perfect guard position, with firing slots already made.

Jim worked up behind the man on duty there. The cowboy was trying to roll a cigarette and swearing each time the tobacco fell out of the paper. Just as the man looked up, Jim's six-gun butt crashed down on his head. Jim tied him securely but with some slack so he could work himself free in two or three hours.

Jim paused at the vantage point and checked the terrain. It was old army training and this time paid off. He spotted a horseman coming along a faint trail that led up to the outpost. It could be a relief guard or a mounted patrol. Jim waited just downwind of the rider until he moved to the lookout area and dismounted. The regular guard was leaning against the snag as if asleep. The new rider jumped down, a snarl on his lips as he headed for the wayward guard. Jim sprang up behind him, tapped him on the shoulder and then smashed the heavy .45 butt over his head.

"Night time," Jim said as the man looked up at him before passing out. Jim tied him, fastened the horse's reins at the spot, and worked back down to where he had left Melinda.

He figured they had an hour to get through the hole he had just punched in the cordon of defenses and into the heart of the Big Stake mine operation. He would check for one more guard, probably in a tree, and somewhere within sight of the mine buildings themselves.

Jim relaxed a moment after working up a steep hill which would bring them down into the mine area from the river side. He hadn't thought about his chest wounds for half the morning. It seemed to cut down on the pain if he simply put it all out of his mind.

"There's a rider coming across above us," Melinda said. She pointed. Jim froze against the tree as the horse walked across their proposed path a hundred feet ahead. When the rider was gone, Jim leaned over and kissed her cheek.

"I just promoted you to head scout," he said.

"I'd rather have another kind of promotion," she said laughing. He watched her eyes, the intensity, the wanting.

"Later," he said, and when he was sure the rider was gone, they moved on down the mountainside.

Ten minutes later they slid over a patch of blue and yellow wildflowers and lay behind a big fallen log. Around the end they could see the mine below, less than two hundred yards away. Jim began checking the trees. Most of the big ones here were lodgepole pine with a few white fir thrown in, but their branches were too thick to make good observation posts. He looked at a dozen alders growing along the river, but none had any men in them. A ten-minute serious study produced no tree-sitting lookout. Jim wasn't satisfied.

"Sit tight, I'm going to scout around. Don't move until I give you a double-arm wave." She nodded and he scurried into the brush on all fours.

Jim was convinced there was another guard, a hidden one. It had worked before when they caught him; they wouldn't change a winning plan. He snaked his way along a brush-covered gulley, always keeping protection over him, until he was less than a hundred yards from the mine buildings. Then Jim turned and looked behind him. He saw the man almost at once. He was twenty feet up in the big ponderosa pine. Most of the branches had been cut away on a six-foot section all around the tree, giving him a fine all-around view at medium and long range. But directly below he was blinded by other branches.

Jim watched the man for five minutes and saw that he never moved. Was he sleeping? Jim wasn't sure, but he did know he couldn't do a thing about taking over the mine until that man with the rifle was disposed of. Jim couldn't think of any way to get him down except by shooting. How was he supposed to capture the man without arousing the whole camp?

Chapter Fifteen

Jim squatted and stared at the sentry. How in hell did he get rid of that man? He pulled a blossom head from a red clover and sucked on the sweet, pink roots as he went over the possibilities. A knife would be best, but there was no clear path for throwing a blade at him. There was no way he could rope the guard at that height, and Jim wasn't going to shoot him out of the tree. Even getting the drop on the man could result in some wild shooting, which would alert the men at the mine.

A sudden whump came from the building below, followed by a cheer and a hiss of steam. Jim knew the new counterfeit coins were being struck. But even the noise didn't wake the sentry.

Jim worked his way back to Melinda and told her exactly what he wanted her to do, then crawled back and moved into position just behind a thick clump of brush ten feet from the base of the sentry's tree and waited.

He heard Melinda coming before he saw her, but when he looked, the guard was still snoring. Jim took the first of a half dozen rocks he had gathered and threw it at the sentry. The rock glanced off a limb and fell back. He tried again. The fourth rock penetrated the heavy limb cover and hit the guard's leg. He jolted awake, his rifle at the ready.

Slowly he looked around, checking his area. He spotted Melinda quickly and smiled, sighted in on her, then, evidently realizing that the intruder was a woman, he lowered his weapon.

He followed her course, and when she was close enough for him to see clearly, he grinned. The man slung his rifle over his back and began climbing down the tree. He stood behind it as Melinda came up. She stopped where Jim told her to and began to cry.

The guard moved out slowly.

"Hey, there, Missy, nothing to worry about. You ain't lost, not no more. I done found you."

Melinda only cried harder, and as she bawled, Jim used the sound as cover to move up behind the guard. His arm lifted the rifle and slammed the stock down, dropping the young man into the carpet of pine needles.

It took Jim only a few moments to tie him, using the guard's own kerchief, belt, and rifle sling. A gag in his mouth completed the job. Then Jim took the rifle and moved with Melinda toward the spot they had selected. Now they could see inside the big building. Jim spotted no more guards around the outside of the stamping structure. He saw the big press, heard it clanking away, saw the jets of steam and the smokestacks which pumped out a continual stream of blue wood smoke. He estimated there were ten men working inside.

At one side he saw a handsome democrat buggy. It looked like the same one Sanderson drove away from town in that morning.

Jim thought about the plant for a minute, thought of the depression in which it sat and the hot furnaces and molten metal. He looked at the river and his weathered face cracked into a grin. He took Melinda's hand and moved with her upstream, then waded across on some half-submerged rocks. There was a considerable volume of water running down the center fork of the American.

His idea was firm in his mind now, and Jim looked for the right spot. He found it less than fifty yards upstream from the edge of the building. It was a sandbar which the water had pushed up, and over which it would pour during a heavy rainfall or during the spring snow melt. Now the water swirled around the loose sand and gravel with only a trickle seeping through to be dried up in the soil below. From that point downstream there was a natural depression which had carried overflow water directly to the foundations of the new building.

Jim motioned to Melinda what he wanted done, and she understood. They began to dig out the sand and loose stones with their hands. Jim found a broken branch which he used like a shovel and soon they had a small stream of water working down the wash toward the new building. The water came faster then, starting to tear away at some of the sandbar it had washed up, and as Jim stood in the foot-wide trench, he worked with a small log he had found. Soon they saw the canal grow into a two-foot river. Jim worked harder now, widening the opening of the canal, making it deeper and wider so more of the chattering, leaping water would be forced down the new route. They saw the new water reach the depression where the stamping plant stood. Slowly the wetness began to build up around the foundations.

Jim found a larger log and used it as a ram, blasting away at the sandbank until he had a stream four feet wide and a foot and a half deep washing down and pooling around the raw-lumber building.

Ten minutes later Jim threw down the log and took Melinda upstream another fifty yards where they could see the mine buildings from behind a fallen pine tree.

They watched the water edging higher and higher. Soon it began to lap at the side door.

"I don't understand," Melinda whispered. "What's this supposed to do, drown them?"

Jim shook his head. "Water and molten metal don't mix. Get the two together and you'll have an explosion that you'll never forget. If enough water gets inside that building and hits the molten metal or the red-hot furnaces, it'll be all over."

A yell went up from inside the building, and almost at the same time a man opened the door and dashed out. A wave of water washed into the plant through the door. Jim drove the man back inside with two carefully placed rifle shots. Another man screamed and ran out the door. Jim let him go. Now a flood of water was growing around the building and pouring through the doors. There was more shouting inside and two shots fired. Then another man rushed out and was shot in the back by a gun in the building. He fell and didn't move.

"They can't stop it now," Jim said. "As soon as that water gets a little higher the whole building is going to blow right over the mountain."

One more man got out a side door and streaked into the woods. Another shot blasted from inside the building.

The explosion came as a surprise to both of them. The intensity was like nothing Melinda had ever experienced. She put her hands over her ears and buried her head in Jim's chest. Jim could only compare it with an ammunition dump exploding; everything went up in one giant roar.

The two windows in the building shattered outward, the doors blew off their hinges, and the whole back wall disintegrated, sending wooden and metal splinters shooting toward the log behind which the pair crouched.

As the roof began to cave inward, another explosion tore through the debris, blasting the roof upward and over the front wall, which was already bulging outward. A third roar shook the remains of the wooden structure, mutilating whatever remained of the walls and boards, machinery and men.

The cold water had contacted the hot metal of a boiler and mushroomed into a shattering thunder of released energy.

Boards, bricks, and parts of machines came down like rain on Jim's position a hundred yards upstream. When the falling objects stopped, Jim and Melinda rose, and Jim led the way to the wreckage scene.

Jim moved in first through a foot of water to the shattered front wall. Inside he found two dead men, one wrapped around a heavy steam engine like a boneless rag doll, his head impaled on an iron pipe entering his forehead and protruding out his back hairline. His eyes stared curiously at Jim. The other man was ripped in half. At the far end of what had been the structure Jim found Sanderson sitting behind the remains of the stamping machine. He waved his short-barreled revolver and kept pulling the trigger on the used chambers. His eyes were glazed, and he gave Jim no argument when he was pulled from the water.

He had been sitting on a low table and now Jim saw his problem. Both of his legs had been blown off, sheared below the knee. The muddy water was dark red. Jim carried him outside and across the small road to dry land, where he put makeshift tourniquets on the legs to stop the blood. He left

Melinda holding one stick and twisting up the cloth.

Jim made three more trips into the wreckage, bringing out wounded. One man's left leg had been struck by flying metal and had a slash to the bone. On dry land Jim stuffed the man's shirt into the wound and tied it tightly with the long sleeves.

When he had brought out all the wounded he could find, Melinda sloshed through the two-foot-deep water.

"The gold, Jim. Where's the gold?" she asked.

Then Jim noticed the sprays of metal that had splashed and blasted in a fine sheen over much of the rubble. It made an intriguing sight, but Jim shrugged it off. It would be too hard to scrape together enough to be practical. Some other metal had splashed around, too, a dull silver color, and Jim decided it must be the core metal for the phony coins.

"Is that all the gold there is?" Melinda asked, her eyes unbelieving.

Jim looked further. The sprays of gold seemed heavier at one end of the wreckage. He probed around the stamping press, pushing aside boards and buckets, tipping over a hand ladle of heavy iron.

Then he went to the bench where he had

found Sanderson. Under it, surrounded by heavy iron weights, he found the edge of a strongbox. The lid had been partially ripped off by some mighty hand. Jim kicked aside some splintered boards and pushed the iron weights away. Soon he could pry open the twisted lid.

"Melinda, come here," Jim said.

She sloshed through the water and over the boards. The water level was still rising. When she looked inside the box she shrieked. Her arms went around him and she hugged him tightly.

The strongbox was filled with gold bars.

"Oh, Jim, how much is all that worth?"

Jim looked at the gold and laughed easily. "I think I have a girl with a bad case of gold fever."

"You bet," Melinda said, her eyes snapping. "Is there ten thousand dollars' worth?"

Jim counted the hoard. There were an even twenty gold bars stacked neatly in the box. He picked one up and hefted it.

"They should be ten-pounders, which means they're worth a little over thirty-three hundred dollars a bar."

Melinda's eyes widened. She gasped and put her hand on the yellow metal. "Sixty-six thousand dollars' worth?"

"Right close."

"Glory!" She looked around. "Let's get this out of here and hid before somebody comes. How about stowing it in that fancy democrat buggy? Sanderson won't be needing it. Then it's back to town or on to San Francisco!"

Jim agreed and for fifteen minutes they carried the gold to the buggy. None of the wounded men were in any shape to question what they were doing. Sanderson rocked on the ground, where he sat singing a little song that made no sense.

By the time they got it all stowed in the carpetbag under the front seat of the buggy, they were soaked to the waist. Jim hoped nobody tried to pick up the carpetbag, since it now weighed over two hundred pounds.

Jim went back into the wrecked building to try to find any of the counterfeit double eagles. He located only three and decided the others they made had been scattered by the explosions.

Two men came riding up. They had been mounted guards and now looked in disbelief at the stamping shed. They didn't even bother to draw their guns. Jim disarmed them and set them to carrying the dead men from the waterlogged wreckage and the surrounding area. They found a wagon that could be used for the injured and hitched up their horses to pull it.

Jim counted up his group. He had two fit men, five wounded, and four dead men stretched out in the noontime sun. He was about to pull away in the buggy when he saw another rider coming in. He stopped and brought his rifle up. Jim was about to fire a warning shot when Melinda touched his sleeve.

"Don't shoot; it's some army man, looks like it could be our captain friend."

CHAPTER SIXTEEN

Jim waited as the army man rode up. It was Captain Davis who stopped beside the buggy and stared at the ruined building.

"My god, it looks like Deep Bottom all over again. What happened, Steel?"

"They resisted."

The captain sent him an amused glance at hearing the old army phrase, then looked at the prisoners and wounded.

"I finally got word what happened in town, then my sergeant said the democrat buggy did head this way, so we got together a detail to come out and take a look. I'll get the wounded on the way to a doctor in town." He turned and gave the orders to two soldiers who galloped up. Then he got down from his mount and gave the horse to an aide.

"You got the dies out, of course?"

"Nope, didn't know where to look."

"On the stamping press, you damn civilian," Davis said with the slightest touch of a grin. "Let's go find them."

Five minutes later they had waded through hip-deep water, and Davis found the dies on the press. On a bench at one side he spotted a wrench and removed the dies from the holders.

"Good as new," he said, examining them. "Any gold left, or did you splatter it all over the damn county?"

"You can scrape it off the walls if you want to, Captain. I decided that was too much work even for gold."

"And so out of the goodness of your civilian heart . . ."

Jim stabbed a look his way. "Yeah, I only got back your dies and saved your whole damn miserable army career for you, besides your neck a couple of times. Now, any more questions?"

Captain Davis shook his head and threw the wrench into the three feet of muddy water. "I'm in a bad position to be asking you anything more, but what happened to Sanderson?"

Jim told him about the man's legs and then about Bert Ronson. They walked together out of the water and back to dry land, then explored the mine cookshack. which hadn't been damaged. The mine cookshack still had plenty of food and a Chinese cook. Captain Davis instructed him to finish his work on the noon meal but to make it for twenty.

Jim, Melinda, and Captain Davis sat on a grassy spot next to the cookhouse and let the sun dry their clothes. The rest of the army detail came riding up and the captain gave orders to the men, posting guards around the site.

After the meal, Jim and Melinda headed for the buggy.

"Captain Davis, sir," Jim said. "Sanderson, the prisoners, and the dies are all yours. It's time I head back for the big city."

The captain shook Jim's hand warmly. "So you're not even going to wait for the reward? You've got a thousand dollars coming."

Jim took off his hat and reset the crown creases.

"Tell you what. I think that reward should go to Ruth Wentz for digging up the story and getting down the facts. The money will help her get another newspaper started in town. Sacramento can use a good paper."

"You serious?"

"Yes. When the cash arrives, just turn it over to her."

"Jim, sure you don't need that thousand good U.S. dollars?"

"Captain, just the honor of helping out the United States Government and one of its loyal army servants is high enough reward for me," Jim said.

Melinda snickered.

The captain didn't quite understand. He said so and quickly added that it might be better if he stayed in the dark about the whole thing.

"Washington has back the dies, we give out the reward, and it's all over. I'll have my men block off that new river you started up there so we can drain the water from the wreck. After that we'll pick up what gold we can find and those counterfeit double eagles. Which might take some time."

Jim noticed the troopers had on field packs, ready for an extended stay.

"We were just leaving," Jim said. "Sounds like too much work around here." He boosted Melinda into the buggy seat. He noticed Melinda kick backward with her shoe to be sure the carpetbag of gold was in place. It was.

"Think you can find your way back to town?" Davis asked, tipping his hat in salute to Melinda.

"Come to think of it, Captain, I'm not in any big hurry," Jim said.

The trail away from the mine followed the

middle fork of the American River downstream, crossed over it after about a mile,
and veered off to the left toward Sacramento. But Jim turned the other way, urg-
ing the white mare across a meadow and
into a small grove of alder near the river.
He drove in until the rig couldn't be seen
from the road, then stopped the horse and
tied the reins.

Melinda leaned against his shoulder and
his arm went around her. The kiss was slow,
luxurious, as if they had the rest of the sum-
mer. Melinda sighed and leaned back in the
seat.

"Nice," she said.

"Very nice," he agreed.

She looked up at him with one eyebrow
arched. "I was thinking about the gold, my
share, thirty-three thousand dollars' worth."

"Who agreed to a fifty-fifty split?"

"You did. Partners right down the
middle." She pretended to punch her elbow
into his injured chest.

"Yeah, fifty-fifty."

"That's your trouble, Steel. No killer
instinct. You've got an honest stripe a mile
wide right down the middle of your back."
She leaned up and kissed him again. "And I
wouldn't have it any other way."

He got down from the buggy and started

to help her, but she suddenly jumped so he had to catch her.

"Hey, let's do that again," she said.

Instead, he carried her to the edge of the river and threatened to throw her in. She calmed down and talked him out of it, then sat beside him on the grass and they threw rocks into the water.

They talked about a lot of things, but not what would happen when they got back to town. Melinda had a vague feeling that it wasn't going to be the same.

She reached up and kissed Jim again, loving his rough, unshaven face, then pulled his hands to her breasts and stretched out in the soft grass.

They made love slowly, softly, exploring, learning more about each other. Afterwards they lay in each other's arms.

"Jim, darling, I've never been happier than I am at this very minute. Why does it have to end?"

"Everything ends, Melinda."

He lifted her up and they waded into the cold mountain stream. Jim's chest, still bandaged, did not show any signs of new blood spills. Melinda sank into the clear water and swam across the deepest part, then came back. They both got out of the water and lay on the grass in the warm sun.

"Jim, we make a good team, you know that?"

"I know."

"So why do we break up a good team?"

"You know me, Melinda. I'm a loner. I don't like a double harness."

"Jim, what other woman do you know with thirty-three thousand dollars in gold who sleeps with you?"

He chuckled. "None." Jim kissed her nose. "Melinda, can you see me tending a town house, working in the front yard, going to town meeting and complaining how the gambling halls and saloons are evils to the upbringing of our children?"

She laughed in spite of her serious mood.

"I've got to move, to roam. I've got to go where the yellow is, whether it's coming out of the ground or taking a long train ride. I've got the gold fever and I'll never get rid of it."

"You don't have to stop. Just take me with you; we make a damn good team."

"Too good, Melinda. We'd stick out like a three-legged bronc everywhere we showed up."

"But I thought that you had some feelings . . ."

He kissed her hard and pulled her on top of him.

"I do, damnit, that's the whole problem. It would be fine for a month, maybe a year, and then you'd want to change me, but I won't and it . . . hell, it just won't work."

She was crying when he lifted her head, tears rolling out of mint-green eyes.

"Jim?"

"Yes."

"If I can't go with you, love me again, right now."

It was after four o'clock when they drove up in front of the hotel. Word of the explosions and the survivors was all over Sacramento. The people had seen the wounded and dead brought in and saw the army bring in Sanderson as a prisoner.

Jim realized that without Sanderson's backing the sheriff wouldn't bother him. Melinda went into the hotel to find Ruth Wentz, and soon she and Jim met in the nearly deserted hotel dining room for coffee.

Ruth faced Jim squarely. "Jim, I don't know how to thank you for what you did this morning. You saved my life for sure. I was so mortified I wanted to die when he ripped my . . . my dress. I haven't had such an experience before."

She paused and took a big breath. "There,

I said it. I never thought I'd be able to." She smiled faintly. "I guess it wasn't so hard at that."

"Ruth, I'm sorry I didn't get there quicker; that was a beautiful dress he ruined," Jim said. Melinda told Ruth what happened at the mine, omitting any mention of the gold bars.

"Mr. Sanderson told us he was ashamed about burning down your newspaper," Jim said. "He decided he should make it up to you, and he gave us two bars of gold for you. Each one weighs ten pounds, and the two are worth six thousand, six hundred dollars. That should get you back in business here with a new shop and new equipment."

Melinda glanced up at Jim quickly. She frowned, but Jim ignored her.

Ruth shook her head. "Somehow I can't believe Mr. Sanderson could be quite so generous."

"Oh, he was a changed man after we caught him with the dies, and he got injured. No reason for you to mention this to him or put it in your new paper. He said it was a secret between the four of us."

"Then it's true? You really mean it?" She looked at Melinda.

"Why, of course. If Jim says it's true, then

it most certainly is."

Ruth jumped up, and as Jim stood she threw her arms around him and hugged him, then kissed him. Jim caught her with his hands and when her lips came away from his, he pulled her closer and kissed her again.

Melinda cleared her throat. "Well, does this mean you two are engaged or something? Kissing in public this way, that's shameful."

Ruth pulled back at once, smiling. "I liked that," she said.

Melinda laughed. "Don't get your hopes up, Ruth. It's time you know that Jim Steel is not the kind to marry and settle down." She waited until the other two had returned to their seats, Jim grinning and Ruth still a little awed by her own forwardness.

"Did I tell you two that I've decided to stay right here in Sacramento and open my own gambling hall? It's not going to be a saloon, but a fancy gambling parlor. Nobody will get inside the door if he wears a gun or if he's in work clothes. Fancy dress only. It's gonna be first-class swanky. We'll cater to respectable women who come with their husbands or fiances. A guy in Denver told me about the places they have like it in Europe. I'll make mine better than those and clear a million dollars and retire in some swanky place in San Francisco."

She looked at the surprised faces. "And I'm offering the job of manager to the only man who can handle it, Jim Steel."

She waited for a moment, then broke up laughing. She looked at Ruth, who began to giggle, then guffaw, and a moment later the two women stood and were holding each other up as they laughed so hard they cried. They both knew he was going to leave town, and that in a way they both had won and lost.

Jim excused himself and went to the buggy and brought inside two bars of gold wrapped in a small cloth sack. He gave the boy guarding the buggy another dollar gold piece and told him not to budge. He told Ruth to deposit the gold with her bank as soon as she could.

Jim left again and took the rest of the gold to the other bank in town, the one Prowl Sanderson didn't own. He put thirty thousand in gold in two separate accounts, one in his name and the other in Melinda's name. He told the banker to weigh the gold carefully and make the deposits firm.

Jim had checked the gold bars. The metal was of slightly varying quality and color, so he knew it had come from at least ten different mines. Probably most of it had been stolen, but Jim had no way of knowing that. He had liberated it from a vile and scandalous criminal and saved the United States Government a lot of trouble. The banker who took it in never questioned it for a moment. He was happy about the deposits. He wrote up the papers and a letter of credit for Jim. Then Jim drew out three hundred dollars in greenbacks.

A half hour later, Jim went back to the hotel and gave Melinda the papers for her share of the gold, then kissed her cheek. He turned and bussed Ruth on a pink cheek and told them both goodbye.

Outside the sun was just going down. His chest started to itch, which meant it was healing. He turned Hamlet out the main street and aimed him toward San Francisco.

Jim had decided to move on to the coast while he was on the trail coming into town four days ago. Maybe he could see a good San Francisco surgeon and have his chest treated so it would heal without scars. It was worth looking into.

Hamlet seemed eager to be on the move again. The big buckskin had been brushed down and given oats and water, and the saddlebags and blanket roll were outfitted for the trail again.

Jim Steel rode down the Sacramento street, wondering what San Francisco would be like. It was a long ride. But his yellow was safely stored away, and it had been over two years since he'd seen the bright lights and the pretty girls of San Francisco.

"Come on, Hamlet, let's go!"

The employees of Thorndike Press hope you have enjoyed this Large Print book. All our Thorndike, Wheeler, and Kennebec Large Print titles are designed for easy reading, and all our books are made to last. Other Thorndike Press Large Print books are available at your library, through selected bookstores, or directly from us.

For information about titles, please call:
(800) 223-1244

or visit our Web site at:
http://gale.cengage.com/thorndike

To share your comments, please write:
Publisher
Thorndike Press
295 Kennedy Memorial Drive
Waterville, ME 04901